THE ONLY WAY

USA TODAY Bestselling Author

Ruth Hartzler

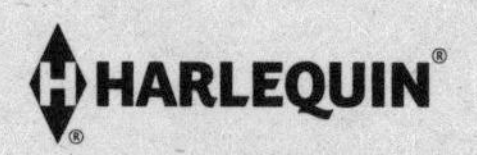

ISBN-13: 978-1-335-46305-0

The Only Way

First published in 2018 by Ruth Hartzler.
This edition published in 2020.

This edition published by arrangement with Harlequin Books S.A.

For questions and comments about the quality of this book, please contact us at CustomerService@Harlequin.com.

Harlequin Enterprises ULC
22 Adelaide St. West, 40th Floor
Toronto, Ontario M5H 4E3, Canada
www.Harlequin.com

Printed in U.S.A.

THE ONLY WAY

Chapter One

One afternoon late in the fall, Rebecca Miller, clothed in a simple dress and prayer *kapp*, stepped out of a taxi on the corner of Penny and Western Avenue. The sunlight, twinkling on the windows of the cafes and restaurants and the automobiles, fell in beams through the trees strung along the sidewalk, dappling the young woman in a playful, yellow light. She was followed out of the taxi by Elijah Hostetler, a tall young man with skin browned by the sun. He paid the driver, before stretching his limbs toward the heavens and yawning.

"Where is the cake store then?" he said, yawning once more.

Rebecca glanced down at the slip of paper where she had penciled the address. "It should be only a block away. We should have asked the taxi to wait for us, but I suppose we can call another one after we pick up the cake."

Rebecca and Elijah were both the youngest of four siblings: Rebecca had three older *schweschders*, and Elijah had three older *bruders*. Through a series of curious and delightful circumstances, Rebecca's oldest *schweschder* had married Elijah's oldest *bruder*; her second oldest *schweschder* had married Elijah's second oldest *bruder*; and, yes, the third oldest *schweschder* had married Elijah's third oldest *bruder*, or she was about to, and that is why Rebecca and Elijah were on an errand to collect the chocolate cake. The other members of their respective families were busy with the wedding preparations, with preparing the food their community would enjoy on the day. Martha, who was to marry Moses, ran a chocolate business, and so a specially made chocolate cake was the obvious choice for one of their wedding cakes.

"Come on," said Rebecca, moving through the crowds of people toward the store where the chocolate wedding cake awaited them. "We need to get back shortly. There's still a lot to do."

Elijah yawned for a third time. "I hope the cake isn't too big. I don't know how we'll get it back in one piece. Do you suppose I can make sure it doesn't topple over? I hope we get a driver who's a little more careful around the corners."

"I wouldn't want to be the person who destroyed Martha's main wedding cake," Rebecca said with a grimace.

"Nonsense," Elijah said, scooting around a young boy who had stopped walking all of a sudden in front of him. "She's lovely. I don't think she would be mad at anyone for anything."

"You didn't have to grow up with her," grumbled Rebecca, who was not feeling very charitable this morning. Each person in their community over the past couple of weeks had stopped to congratulate her on the marriage of Martha and Moses, and then each person who stopped her remarked how she would be marrying Elijah next. She knew it was not Elijah's fault that these comments were being made, but she felt irrationally annoyed with him all the same. The fact their *familyes* had sent them on an errand to collect a chocolate cake together would only set more tongues wagging.

"Why are you in a bad mood?" Elijah asked her.

"Stop being so perceptive."

"I'm sorry," he replied, clearly injured by her bad mood. "I'll stop worrying about your feelings, if it would make you feel better?"

Rebecca sighed. "I'm sorry." She took a deep breath and let it out slowly, watching the sun playing on the buildings and trying to calm herself. "Can I be honest with you?"

"Sure."

"I'm a bit annoyed that everyone believes you and I will be married next."

"The idea of marrying me annoys you?"

"Yes," said Rebecca at once. "No. Wait. Sorry, I didn't mean that."

Elijah laughed. "I'd be an amazing husband. What are you even talking about?"

"Sorry!" Rebecca replied. "We shouldn't even be having this conversation."

"It's a great conversation." Elijah chuckled. "Come now. List all the reasons why you don't want to marry me. I can think of a few why I don't want to marry you. You're clearly not a morning person, and you find errands to collect chocolate cakes tedious. Chocolate cakes! They're one of the happiest things in the world."

"You're too smart for your own good," said Rebecca. "That's one reason. And you're a morning person. That's another reason."

"We both have two reasons not to marry each other," said Elijah. The pair now stood pressed up against a building to avoid the crowd of people bustling by, while they searched the numbers on the buildings for the chocolate store. "Are we even?"

"I am sure there are other reasons. I know: you're too good looking. Half the girls I know want to marry you. You are, after all, the last unwed Hostetler *bruder*."

"You would think my charm and good looks were a reason for marrying me, not a reason against."

Rebecca snorted. "You're arrogant."

"*Nee*, confident," replied Elijah. "That's another reason for marrying me. I'm beginning to think you should marry me, after all."

"And we never agree on anything. That's another reason. We should write a list and hand it out to everyone who comes up to me, suggesting you and I should marry."

"That sounds very time consuming. We wouldn't have time to help out with Martha and Moses' wedding if we were to do that." Elijah stroked his chin. "But it's not a bad idea, now that you mention it."

Rebecca smiled. All of Elijah's teasing had shifted her bad mood, and now she was appreciating the rare fall sunlight, the happiness of her older *schweschders*, and the feeling of extraordinary things on the horizon.

"All right," she announced. "You can stop teasing me now. I'm in a better mood. *Denki* for cheering me up."

"Anytime," said Elijah. "Look." He pointed to a small store wedged between two taller buildings. "That's where we need to collect the chocolate cake."

"Good spotting." Rebecca moved toward the small building, pausing in front of it for a moment. "Just so we're clear: you'd make a great husband, but I don't think you'd make a great husband for me."

"We should make each other a deal," said Elijah, "to stop our *familyes* trying to push us into something we both don't want."

"So we're agreed," Rebecca said, her hand hovering above the door handle. "We won't marry each other, no matter how much our *familyes* might wish it, and no matter how many people come up to us, telling us we're next."

"Agreed," Elijah said, firmly.

Chapter Two

Rebecca and her older *schweschders,* Hannah, Esther, and Martha, sat in front of the fire, happily sewing dresses for Martha's upcoming wedding to Moses. There was a new addition to the *familye*, the young lady Sarah Beachy, whom Martha had met in prison when she, Martha, had been falsely arrested for theft while on her *rumspringa.* It was to this matter that the conversation now turned.

"It was so kind of your parents to take me in," Sarah said to the Miller *schweschders*, "with me being a stranger and from a community in another state."

"Yes, it's weird that *Mamm* likes you," Rebecca said.

Hannah gasped. "Rebecca, that's rude! Apologize at once."

Rebecca chuckled. "I didn't mean anything by it, Sarah. It's just that *Mamm* doesn't usually like anyone, but she really likes you. That is what's weird—it's out of character for her."

Surprise was stamped all over Sarah's face. "I can't imagine your *mudder* not liking anyone."

All the girls chuckled at that. Mrs. Miller was not the warmest personality, and tended to hold a grudge, yet she had welcomed Sarah with open arms. Rebecca found this quite strange, and wondered if her *mudder* had known Sarah's *familye* at some point. It was not the way her *mudder* usually acted.

Her *schweschders* would not comment in front of Sarah, so Rebecca turned her attention back to the sewing. "Why are we making purple dresses, Martha?"

"It's for my wedding, of course, Rebecca."

Rebecca groaned dramatically. "Obviously! What I mean is, why is it purple? Hannah had purple dresses for her wedding, and Esther had purple dresses for her wedding."

"I like purple," all three *schweschders* said at once, and then burst out laughing.

"So do I," Rebecca said, "but if I ever get married, I will wear a blue dress, just to be different. Oh, I saw that," she added, when Hannah, Esther, and Martha exchanged glances.

Martha raised her eyebrows. "And I suppose you're not going to marry Elijah Hostetler, just to be different?"

Before Rebecca could answer, Sarah spoke up. "It is quite unusual that all three of you *schweschders* married three *bruders*."

"It will be four soon," Martha said, clearly intent upon teasing Rebecca.

Rebecca raised her hands. "Please stop teasing me

about Elijah. I will *not* be marrying him, don't you understand? It's not nice when you keep teasing me about him." One look at her *schweschders* was enough to tell her that they *were* going to continue to tease her. Rebecca sighed loudly.

"Well, you can't *not* marry him just to be different," Martha said, "especially if he's the love of your life."

Rebecca was growing exasperated. "He's not the love of my life. Anyway, stop trying your matchmaking! You're getting as bad as *Mamm*." She stood up and went over to the fire, and popped on another small log. "It's awfully cold for late November. *Daed* says it might snow tonight." Rebecca hoped her change of subject would be successful. Just to make sure, she added yet another change of subject. "Perhaps Sarah likes Elijah."

Sarah laughed. "*Nee*, leave me out of it, Rebecca. I don't think I will ever get married. I'll be an old maid, and be surrounded by lots of cats." As if on cue, Tom, a fat ginger cat with a big white spot under his chin, walked over to her from his comfortable spot near the fire and purred against her legs. "Look at us, a couple of strays."

Mrs. Miller had never allowed her *dochders* to have pets, saying that animals must earn their keep, but when the stray cat had turned up on the Millers' doorstep just after Sarah had, Mrs. Miller had told Sarah she could keep him. Mrs. Miller had even told Mr. Miller to take him to the veterinarian to be neutered. The cat was even allowed inside. That had very much surprised all her *dochders*, who figured collectively that Mrs. Miller must be getting soft as she grew older. It especially surprised Mary, who had not been allowed to keep Pirate, the stray dog. Still, Mary conceded that cat was a lot less trouble than a dog.

"You're part of our *familye* now, Sarah," Esther said. "Our growing *familye*," she added.

Sarah smiled. "When I see *bopplin* as cute as your *dochder*, Esther, and your twins, Hannah, I do feel I'd like to get married."

Esther rubbed her hands together nervously. "That reminds me, I hope *Mamm* is doing okay with Isobel. I haven't been away from her for so long before."

Hannah moved to reassure Esther. "*Mamm* will be fine with Isobel, and with Rose and Mason too. Actually, she'll be better with Isobel than the twins, as they're into everything now that they're walking."

Rebecca yawned loudly, and everyone looked at her. "Are you tired, Rebecca, or is it just the warmth of the fire making you yawn?" Sarah asked.

Rebecca shrugged. "A bit of both. Working at the B&B can be tiring at times. Anyway, Sarah, you and Mary are doing all the chores with *Mamm* now that I'm at the B&B most days. They're probably equally tiring."

Sarah smiled, and Rebecca studied her face. Sarah was very pretty, with long, straight blonde hair and vivid blue eyes. Her complexion was all peaches and cream. *It's a wonder that a young mann hasn't asked her on a buggy ride yet*, Rebecca thought, her stomach clenching at the thought that Elijah might just be the young *mann* to do so.

"I'll get used to it," Rebecca continued, to take her

mind off her thoughts. "The Flickingers are a lovely couple. I see a lot more of Ida than Samuel, though."

"*Mamm's* not happy that they bought a *haus* so close to ours," Martha volunteered, "what with the cars and *Englischer* traffic that now go past our *haus* on their way to the B&B."

"They don't exactly go right past our *haus*," Rebecca said.

Martha rubbed her forehead. "True, but it's close enough to upset *Mamm*."

Two miles away would be close enough to upset Mamm, Rebecca thought, but kept her opinion to herself. The B&B was only a ten-minute walk away from the Millers' *haus*, in the opposite direction to Noah and Hannah's.

Rebecca was excited that a B&B had opened just up the road, and was glad to see that the old Mennonite building had been renovated. It was wonderful to have new people in the community. That hadn't happened for as long as she could remember, apart from Sarah and Mary. That was the reason that she had accepted the job working at the B&B, helping with the cooking and cleaning. It got her out of the *haus* and into the company of other people. Rebecca had no desire to start her own business like Martha had, but she did want to be around other people, and new people at that.

Chapter Three

Rebecca was pinning sheets to the line, enjoying the late fall sunshine. *It's a good drying day*, she thought. Everyone was predicting an early winter, and a harsh winter at that. Rebecca was already looking forward to spring. It was not that she minded the cold; in fact she preferred winter for the beautiful sights, but she missed the fragrance of all the spring flowers. Spring was always a delight to Rebecca, with the spicy scent of the dianthus, the sweet scent of the honeysuckle, the delicate scent of the hyacinths, and the leathery, earthy fragrance of the saffron. Rebecca had made some lavender spray to put on the linen for the B&B, but nothing could replace the fragrance of fresh spring flowers.

The B&B had electricity thanks to numerous solar panels, and had a large electric washing machine, a far cry from the old wringer washer that Rebecca was used to. "I'm going to have an electric washing machine and solar power when I have my own *haus*," Rebecca said aloud. "I can't go back to the old wringer washer after this."

"That's the first sign of madness, isn't it?"

Rebecca's hands flew to her throat and she looked around to find the source of the male voice. When she saw him, her mouth fell open. Standing in front of her was a tall, young *mann* with black hair and piercing brown eyes, and more to the point, he was covered with tattoos, and wearing a large hoop earring in each ear, and more disturbingly, a large nose ring.

"What is?" she stammered.

"Talking to yourself." The young *mann* laughed and walked closer to her. Rebecca involuntarily took a step backward. "Talking to yourself is the first sign of madness," he said.

"Sorry, no smoking allowed." Rebecca pointed to the cigarette hanging out of his mouth. She felt silly after she said it, but it was an automatic response.

The man simply looked amused by her comment, but continued to smoke. "And who might you be?"

"I'm Rebecca Miller," she said, again without thinking. Annoyed with herself, she added sternly, "Not that it's any of your business. Who are you?"

"Nash Grayson." The man held out a hand.

Rebecca looked at the hand for a moment before shaking it briefly. "I'll find Mrs. Flickinger if you'd like to check in."

The man seemed amused by that comment too, but merely said, "She knows I'm here. I've already checked in."

Rebecca suddenly felt uneasy standing outside the

B&B, talking to a strange man. “I have to go speak to her anyways,” she said, and hurried off. When Rebecca reached the kitchen, Mr. Flickinger was standing behind Mrs. Flickinger, patting her on the shoulder. Mrs. Flickinger had her head down on the large kitchen table. When Mr. Flickinger saw Rebecca, he nodded to her and left the room.

Rebecca hurried over to Mrs. Flickinger and saw that her eyes were swollen. “Are you all right?”

When there was no reply, just an anguished look accompanied by sniffing, Rebecca hurried to make a cup of tea, which she set in front of Mrs. Flickinger.

“Thank you, dear,” Ida Flickinger managed to say, and then she added, “Please sit down.” Rebecca sat next to Ida, who put her hands over Rebecca’s. “There’s something I have to tell you, dear.”

Rebecca nodded and waited patiently.

“My son has just moved back home with us.”

Rebecca momentarily wondered why a son’s return would make a *mudder* cry rather than be happy.

“I’ll have to introduce him to you. Now, Rebecca, he’s not like you’d expect. Samuel and I are very upset about Eli. Oh, he doesn’t call himself Eli anymore…” Ida dabbed at her eyes and gulped. “He calls himself Nash Grayson now.”

Rebecca gasped. “What?” she said. “But I just met him outside. Is he, err, is he your son?”

Ida burst into tears and Rebecca was at a loss how to comfort her. She sat and waited until the sobs subsided. The Amish usually bore their grief silently; Nash must have really upset his *mudder* for her to make such an outward show of emotion.

"He went on *rumspringa*," Ida said, "and then he never came back. He got wilder and wilder. He got a job with *Englischers*, but then he lost all his money gambling on race horses, and now he has tattoos."

Yes, Rebecca thought, *I noticed that, they're hard to miss, seeing that he's covered with them*. Rebecca wished she could think of something to say to comfort Mrs. Flickinger. She thought of saying *He seems nice*, but that sounded too lame, and besides, it wasn't even true.

Ida Flickinger dabbed at her eyes with a handkerchief. "We left our community and came here, as we hadn't heard from Eli for ages. I'm glad he's all right, of course, but he's changed so much."

"But he's staying with you," Rebecca said. "Surely that means he's pleased to see you, and perhaps he will even join the community."

"*Nee*, *nee*, Eli must have other reasons for being here. By the way, my *mudder* knows about him being back, so you don't need to keep it from her. Anyway, *denki*, Rebecca, but I must get back to work. Would you take a cup of peppermint tea up to *Grossmammi* Deborah, and then prepare the Broken Star Quilt room for Eli?"

"*Jah*, of course. I'll do it right now."

The rooms were named after quilt patterns: the Spinning Star Quilt room, the Flower Basket Quilt room, the Log Cabin Quilt room, and the Medallion Quilt room, as well as the Broken Star Quilt room. Each bed had the appropriate quilt, or quilts in the case of multiple beds in the one room, in the room of the same name.

First, Rebecca took up a cup of hot peppermint tea to the room of Mrs. Flickinger's *mudder*, who was known to Rebecca as *Grossmammi* Deborah. *Grossmammi* had been quite ill and was not doing any better, although the *doktor* had her on medication which ensured she was kept comfortable. He had warned the *familye* that she did not have long for this world. Today, *Grossmammi* was fast asleep. Rebecca whispered her name, and when she did not wake up, Rebecca panicked for a moment, until she saw her steady but shallow breathing. Rebecca tiptoed out of the room. She would see if she was awake later.

There were already fresh sheets on the double bed in the Broken Star Quilt room, so Rebecca set herself to vacuuming the blue-gray carpet. This was the plainest room, and the room least used, of all the rooms at the B&B, and Rebecca figured that Ida had chosen it for this reason. Perhaps she wanted her son to remember his early home life, or perhaps it was simply that this room was the least likely to appeal to *Englisch* tourists. The only color in the room was provided by the deep blue and burgundy of the quilt itself. The blinds were white, matching the walls, and the curtains were a dull brown-beige.

Rebecca unplugged the vacuum cleaner and dusted the plain oak dresser.

"No television?"

Rebecca spun around to see Nash Grayson, or Eli Flickinger as she now knew him to be, standing in the doorway. He placed his suitcases down and crossed the room to her. "No television?" he repeated. "And what about Wi-Fi?"

Rebecca's mouth ran dry. She wished she could lecture this ungrateful young man about upsetting his *mudder*, but instead she simply said, "*Nee*. What do you expect? This is an Amish *haus*." Rebecca felt bad for lying, but if his mother hadn't told him about the available Wi-Fi, then why should she?

"*Nee*," Nash said, exaggerating the word, "it is not, it is an Amish *business*, and as you know, electricity is usually permitted in Amish businesses, so why no Wi-Fi or television?"

Rebecca shrugged. "You would have to ask your *mudder*. I assume guests here know it's an Amish business, so they expect an Amish experience. Anyway, if you don't like it, you can always leave." Rebecca thought perhaps she should not speak in this manner to her employer's son, but he rubbed her the wrong way.

"What, and miss out on the free food?"

Rebecca shot a sharp look at Nash to see if he was joking, and he was smiling, although she had no idea how to read him. He winked at her and left the room. *He's a little dangerous*, Rebecca thought, but the thought excited her. Like her two oldest *schweschders*, Hannah and Martha, Rebecca had no desire to go on *rumspringa*. Martha had, and look where it had gotten her, falsely arrested and in prison, which is where she had met Sarah Beachy, also on *rumspringa*. Noah Hostetler had been on *rumspringa* when he was driving the car that had hit their buggy. And look what *rumspringa* had done to Nash Grayson!

Nee, I won't be going on rumspringa, Rebecca thought, but at the same time she could not help but be drawn to Nash. He seemed exciting, and that to her was exhilarating, after what she considered was her dull and boring life. She did want a little excitement in her life, just not too much.

Nash watched Rebecca shut the door to his room, and turned to survey his surroundings. Boring, plain, and dull, just like his childhood. He bet his mother had given him the worst room at the B&B just to spite him. You would think a mother would want to support her own son, but no, this was the way she treated him.

Oh well, at least I'm getting free room and board, he consoled himself. *It's the least my parents can do for me.* Besides, there was the potential for excitement in the person of Rebecca Miller.

Nash thought Rebecca was the prettiest girl he had seen in long time, and he liked the natural look on girls. He had never gotten used to too much make-up, despite living as an *Englischer* for some time. Perhaps he could convince Rebecca to leave the community for him. That would have the added benefit of upsetting his parents. After all, they had refused to lend him the money to pay off his gambling debts. What sort of parents were they! Nash threw down his largest suitcase on the bed in disgust.

Chapter Four

When Rebecca arrived home from working at the B&B that night, she thought she saw the bishop driving away from her house.

She hurried inside. "*Mamm*, was that the bishop's buggy?"

"And *hullo* to you, Rebecca," her mother snapped. "I'm sure I raised you well enough to know you should greet me before making idle conversation."

"Sorry, *Mamm*," Rebecca said. "*Hullo*, *Mamm*. I hope you had a pleasant day?"

Her mother glared at her. "Now, there's no need to be sarcastic, Rebecca."

Rebecca resisted rolling her eyes. Sometimes there was just no winning with her mother. "I'm sorry, *Mamm*," she said meekly.

Her words seemed to satisfy Mrs. Miller. "Yes, that was the bishop, and he came to tell us that the Flickingers' son, Eli, has just arrived in town. The bishop was on his way to visit the Flickingers and I asked him to invite them here for dinner tonight."

Rebecca's jaw fell open. "Who exactly did you invite for dinner tonight?"

The mother stomped her foot. "Honestly, Rebecca. Haven't you listen to a word I said? I only just told you that I've asked the bishop to invite the Flickingers for dinner."

"And their son, Eli?" Rebecca asked.

"Of course. It would be rude to invite Samuel and Ida Flickinger and not invite their son, Eli. I'm sure he is a most pleasant young man. Sarah, Mary, and you can help me prepare dinner."

"But *Mamm*," Rebecca began, but her mother had already walked into the kitchen.

Rebecca wondered what she should do. Clearly she needed to warn her mother about Nash, but if the bishop hadn't seen fit to do so, should she? She wasn't sure. After some consideration, she decided she should speak with her father.

"Where are you going, Rebecca?" her mother called, after Rebecca left the kitchen.

"I need to ask *daed's* advice."

Mrs. Miller put her hands on her hips. "Why? You can't ask my advice?"

"Sorry, *Mamm*," Rebecca said as she hurried out the door. When she reached the barn, in which her father ran his furniture making business, she waited until her father had stopped what he was working on. He looked up and saw her. "Rebecca," he said. "What brings you?"

"I just arrived home and saw the bishop driving

away," she told him. "The bishop told *Mamm* that the Flickingers' son arrived today. *Mamm* invited the three of them for dinner and the bishop's on his way to the B&B now to invite them."

"That's *gut*," her father said.

Rebecca shook her head. "*Nee*, *Datt*. I met Eli Flickinger today. He has left the community. He is an *Englischer* now."

Her father frowned. "And the bishop didn't tell your mother?"

"I don't think so," Rebecca said, frowning. "Anyway, Eli calls himself Nash. He is covered in tattoos and he was smoking when I met him."

"It's not our place to judge," Mr. Miller said. "'There is but one lawgiver and judge, who is able to save and to destroy, who are you to judge another?'"

Rebecca allowed herself a small smile. Her father loved to quote Scripture, but not in front of his wife or other members of the community, as they would accuse him of being *Scripture smart*, prideful for having the knowledge to quote Scripture.

"It's just that I think *Mamm* will be upset when she meets him."

"I'm sure the bishop has his reasons," her father said. "Besides, it wouldn't be the first time we have had *Englischers* at our table."

"Okay." With that, Rebecca went back to the kitchen. Her father did not seem at all concerned, so she didn't think she should be either. After all, the bishop knew more than she did, and maybe he had a plan for Nash.

Still, Rebecca could not help feeling that Mrs. Flickinger would be embarrassed.

And she was right. Mrs. Miller, Rebecca, Sarah, and Mary had prepared roasted chicken, roast beef, mashed potatoes, gravy, and pot pie, along with vegetables for dinner.

Rebecca had not had a chance to pull Mary or Sarah aside and tell them what she knew about Nash Grayson. Mr. Miller, however, was home early for dinner and Rebecca knew that was because of her words. Rebecca had only just finished stirring the chicken chunks in the pot pie when she heard a buggy arrive. *This will be interesting*, she thought with a grimace.

Mr. Miller showed Mr. and Mrs. Flickinger into the house. Mr. Flickinger's face was white and drawn, and Mrs. Flickinger continually wrung her hands. Behind them was a silent Nash. Rebecca noted that her mother's eyes popped out of her head at the sight of Nash. Her hands flew to her throat and her jaw worked up and down like a goldfish's.

"*Hullo, hullo, hullo*," Mrs. Miller sputtered. "How nice to see you, Samuel and Ida. I'm so glad you could make it, and Eli, how nice to meet you."

"My name is Nash," he said through narrowed eyes.

Mrs. Flickinger wrung her hands even harder. She then clutched the sides of her apron with both hands and dug her fingernails in.

"Please come inside and have some meadow tea before dinner," Mrs. Miller said. She ushered them into the living room. "Would you like some meadow tea or something else to drink?" she asked Nash.

"Yes, whiskey please," he said.

Mrs. Miller forced a laugh. "Oh, the humor of the *youngie* these days." She followed her words with a sharp glare at Nash and then left the room.

Mr. Miller did his best to make conversation. "So, Eli, you just arrived in town today?"

"It's Nash," Nash spat.

Mr. Miller tried again. "So, Nash, you arrived in town today?" he asked him again.

"Yes," Nash said. He then turned his attention to Sarah and Mary. Rebecca noted that both girls could hardly keep their eyes off Nash. They seemed equally shocked at the sight of him.

"Are you Rebecca's sisters?" he asked them.

"No, I'm a friend of Martha's," Sarah said. "I'm living with the Miller *familye*."

Eli looked Mary up and down. "And who are you then?" he asked bluntly.

"I'm Mary. I'm not anyone's *schweschder*. Actually, I am. Oh, I mean I'm not an only child, because I have a *bruder*. As a matter of fact, I'm not from this community. I came here not long after the buggy accident to help Mrs. Miller with the girls, but now they've all gone off and got married. Well, two of them are married and one of them will be soon. That only leaves Rebecca here to get married. Anyways, I liked it so much here that I stayed on. I live in the *grossmammi haus* out the back. There used to be a woman living out there with me. Her name was Linda and she was only living there because her *familye's* house burnt down, but everyone rebuilt the house and Linda moved out. I have a dog called Pirate, but he lives at David Yoder's house. Actually I half-own him."

To Rebecca's surprise, Nash seemed to be hanging on every word. She knew Mary must be nervous, because she always talked non-stop when she was anxious.

"Whose cat is that?" Nash said, spying Sarah's ginger cat.

"He's my cat," Sarah said.

"I like cats. They're nicer than people. I don't like people," Nash said. He almost spat the words.

Throughout the conversation, Mrs. Flickinger's face had grown more and more distressed. Her husband patted her on the shoulder from time to time, but it didn't seem to help.

"Samuel, have you heard about the Widow Ramseyer's buggy horse?" Mr. Miller asked Mr. Flickinger in a loud voice. Before Mr. Flickinger could respond, he added, "The mare has arthritis in the knee, so Rhoda had to retire her. She got the x-ray results only this morning. Mrs. Graber has prepared liniments for the mare's knee as well as herbs for Rhoda to give the mare, so she will be fine but will live out her days in the fields. Rhoda is left without a buggy horse."

Mrs. Miller returned, holding a tray of steaming mugs. "Why did you not tell me this, Abraham?"

"I just did," he said with a grin.

Mrs. Miller scowled at him. "That is not *gut*. Rhoda cannot afford a reliable horse. What will she do, living by herself? She has no *kinner* to look after her. Have you told the bishop?"

"I only just found out," Mr. Miller said. "I hear the

bed and breakfast business is doing very well. Is that so, Ida?"

Rebecca smiled at the way her father managed to change the subject.

"*Jah*, it is." Mrs. Flickinger brightened up, albeit ever so slightly.

Mr. Miller nodded. "I've always thought a bed and breakfast would be an interesting business. I might have tried it myself if I hadn't gone into the business of furniture making. I don't know if my wife would have enjoyed it though."

"Enjoyed what?" she asked him.

"Running a B&B," Mr. Miller replied placidly.

"I don't have the patience for that," she said. "Surely, it is hard to deal with the public?" She addressed the question to Mrs. Flickinger.

"Yes, it is at times," Ida said in a small voice. "Thank you so much for inviting us for dinner."

"I'm so happy you could come," Mrs. Miller said.

Nash yawned loudly and looked around the room. "Do you normally have dinner so late?" he asked Mrs. Miller.

Rebecca couldn't believe the rudeness of the man.

"We're having dinner soon," Mrs. Miller said in even tones. Rebecca realized her mother was doing her best to be nice to Nash, so as not to upset his parents. She figured this was going to be quite an awkward dinner.

After they were seated at the dinner table and had all bowed their heads for the silent prayer, Rebecca opened one eye. She saw Nash grab a bagel and stick it inside his shirt. She shut her eyes quickly.

“Come, Ida, please eat,” Mrs. Miller said after a few minutes.

Mrs. Flickinger sniffled. “I’m sorry, Rachel. I just don’t feel terribly hungry tonight.”

“Nonsense,” Mrs. Miller said. “You need to eat to keep up your strength. Otherwise, it will be hard for you to run that business. It must be very hard work to run a business such as yours.”

“It is,” Ida agreed.

Rebecca thought Mrs. Flickinger was brightening up and figured it was because Nash hadn’t done anything outrageous for a few minutes.

Nash ate greedily, and Rebecca wondered if he had not had enough money to eat properly in recent times. Maybe that explained his bad mood. In fact, she was surprised at the amount of food he consumed. She noticed that when he thought nobody was looking, he put food in his pockets.

Mr. Flickinger hardly said a word throughout dinner. Mr. Miller finally managed to engage Mr. Flickinger in conversation about the B&B business, and everyone around the table seemed to relax a little. By the time the women served dessert, Rebecca thought the night was turning out better than she had thought it would.

When she sat down after serving dessert, Nash turned his attention to her. “What do you do for fun around here?”

“There’s the Singing,” she began, but he wrinkled his nose in obvious disgust. “And then there’s volleyball after the meetings,” Rebecca continued. “And there’s horse riding, and some of the *menner* go fishing or hunting. At night we play board games or read, or maybe sew."

"How do you stand so much excitement?" Nash said snarkily.

Rebecca shot him a glare in response.

"You're not a very nice person, are you?" Mary said. "You remind me of David Yoder when I first met him. He wasn't a very nice person either, but he's improved. In fact, he's quite a nice person now. I'm surprised you said something rude after being invited for dinner at someone else's house. Maybe you should be rude only in your own house."

Everyone looked shocked at Mary's words. It took Rebecca a while to remember Mary had spoken that way to David Yoder when she had first met him. She hadn't heard Mary speak to anyone like that since, but then again, she couldn't recall that Mary had met anyone rude since then.

Nash took a while to recover from his shock. "I haven't met an Amish girl who was so outspoken before." Still, Rebecca thought his words held admiration. She noted that her mother was secretly pleased at Mary's words. Even Mrs. Flickinger had the ghost of a smile tugging at the corners of her lips.

"So, I've been told, haven't I?" Nash continued with a laugh. "Remind me not to cross you again, Martha."

"My name is Mary," she said. "Martha is Rebecca's sister and she is marrying Moses soon."

Nash waved one hand in the air in dismissal. "Mary, Martha—who cares? They both start with M. All these religious names!" he huffed. "Honestly, I don't know why the Amish don't call their children interesting names like Tiffany or Augustus. There are just so many Biblical names, aren't there, and everyone gets called the same names: Matthew, Mark, Luke, John. No wonder I was confused. Surely it isn't a sin to be original?"

Mr. Flickinger opened his mouth as if to rebuke him, but Mr. Miller spoke first. "You do have a good point, Nash. It *is* confusing. Why, we have several Abrahams in the community and several Rachels too. It does get confusing."

Rebecca considered that her parents were being very nice to Nash. If it was her house, she would have kicked him out long ago. He had to be the most obnoxious person she had ever met. There was simply no excuse for his rudeness.

The Flickinger and the Miller *familyes* sat around drinking coffee after dinner, although it was plain to Rebecca that they wanted to leave as fast as they could to save further embarrassment by Nash. Rebecca was surprised when Nash spoke politely. "This is good coffee. Thank you, Mrs. Miller."

Mrs. Miller appeared shocked that he'd thanked her. "Why, you're quite welcome," she said. Rebecca noticed that Mrs. Miller had not once met Nash's eyes, but continued to stare at the tattoos all over his arms.

"Does it hurt?" Mary said.

Nash looked up. "What? Does what hurt?"

"The ring in your nose," she said. "Is it there as a punishment?"

"Punishment?" Nash appeared confused. "What do you mean, is it a punishment?"

"I don't know why you should have to wear it," Mary continued. "Our neighbor's bull kept getting out, so he put a ring in his nose so he could lead him back."

Nash clutched his sides and laughed hard. Finally, he recovered. "No. Lots of men wear nose rings now," he told Mary.

"But why?" Mary persisted.

Nash seemed at a loss. "Well, um, it looks good," he said.

Mary's jaw dropped open. "It looks good? Oh I see, this must be an English thing." She nodded slowly as she said it.

Nash continued to look shocked, and Rebecca smiled to herself. Nash had certainly met his match in Mary.

Chapter Five

The four Hostetler *bruders*, Noah, Jacob, Moses, and Elijah, were sitting around the table in the Hostetler farm kitchen, enjoying a hearty lunch of meat, potatoes and gravy, salad and vegetables, followed by thick chunks of apple pie. They had finally finished a section of fencing that had taken much of their time the past few weeks, and all were in good spirits.

Elijah was staring absently at the table, which he and his *bruders* had made for their *mudder* some years ago, with help from Mr. Miller. It was made from thick planks of boards they had salvaged from a local, old tobacco barn, and Mr. Miller had helped them attach breadboard ends using mortise and tenon joints. The *bruders* had been concerned about the nail holes and saw marks, but Mr. Miller had told them that the distressed and weathered look was prized by *Englischers*. At any rate, their *mudder* had liked it, and that was all that mattered.

"What are you thinking about, Elijah?" Noah asked, and Elijah looked up into the laughing faces of his *bruders*.

"Thinking about Rebecca again?" Moses teased.

Jacob chimed in. "You know, soon your three *bruders* will be married to Rebecca's three *schweschders*. It's only natural that you and Rebecca are next to be married."

"Haa, haa, haa, that's the first time I've heard that joke before," Elijah said with mock seriousness.

Noah stopped spooning food into his mouth for a moment and lay down his fork. "Seriously, Elijah, all jokes aside, when are you going to ask Rebecca to marry you?"

Elijah let out a long breath. "I don't know how she feels about me."

"She loves you," all three *bruders* said in unison.

Elijah held up his hand. "I don't know that. We're the best of friends, and have been for as long as I can remember, but what if she only sees me as a friend? I'm worried that she's just going to fall into marrying me, from the pressure of everyone's expectations."

"Why don't you just ask her to marry you and see what she says?" Jacob asked.

Elijah's stomach churned. He could not bear the thought of Rebecca turning him down. On the other hand, what if she accepted just because it was the thing to do? "My concern is," Elijah said aloud, "that Rebecca would marry me, but not out of any deep love for me, but just because we're *gut* friends and everyone expects it of us."

Noah cut himself a large piece of apple pie before he asked, "Would that be so bad?"

"Of course it would be bad," Elijah said, a little frustrated.

Noah waved his hand at him. "You didn't let me finish. Love could come later, after marriage. You two are well suited."

Elijah groaned. "The three of you were all in love before you were married." The three *bruders* nodded. "So why should it be different for me?" he asked.

Moses and Jacob just shrugged. "The thing is," Noah said, "that you should ask yourself how long you are prepared to wait."

Elijah had to admit that Noah had a valid point. "I don't really know," he said. "I keep hoping I'll have some sign from Rebecca about how she feels about me, but she never gives me any clues."

"You do want *kinner*, don't you?" Noah asked.

Elijah was surprised at the question. "*Jah*, of course I do."

"Well, you'd better propose to Rebecca sometime within the next few decades," Noah said, and the three *bruders* laughed.

Elijah shook his head. He was a little irritated that everyone made remarks about him marrying Rebecca, and his *bruders* were no help at all.

At that moment, his *mudder*, Katie Hostetler, walked into the kitchen. *At least Mamm takes me seriously and doesn't tease me*, Elijah thought.

"What are you doing home at this time, *Mamm*?" Noah asked.

"I left a quilt I've been working on here and a customer wants to see it," she explained. "What are you boys all talking about?"

The four *menner* exchanged glances, and their *mudder* looked from one to the other. "Is it a secret?"

Elijah sighed. "*Nee, Mamm.* My *bruders* have been encouraging me to ask Rebecca to marry me."

"I'm pleased to hear it," Katie Hostetler said, much to Elijah's surprise, and Noah, Jacob, and Moses all chuckled. "I didn't want to be an interfering *mudder*, which is why I haven't said anything before," she continued, "but Elijah, how long are you going to wait? What if Rebecca is asked on a date by another *mann*?"

"She doesn't like any of the *menner* in the community, *Mamm*," Elijah said.

"Well, perhaps that is true, but there is a new *mann* now. The Flickingers' son has just returned to the community and he's on *rumspringa*. Some girls find adventurous young *menner* on *rumspringa* attractive. How long are you going to wait to ask Rebecca to marry you, Elijah?"

Elijah simply groaned and put his head in his hands, while his three *bruders* all chuckled.

Chapter Six

"Here you are, finally!" Mrs. Miller exclaimed as soon as Rebecca walked into the house after finishing her work for the day at the B&B.

"What is it, *Mamm*?"

"We are taking Mary to see that dog, Pirate," Mrs. Miller said.

"Why isn't Mary going by herself?" Rebecca regretted the words as soon as they were out of her mouth. She knew her mother had a reason for everything she did, and this was obviously one of her mother's plots.

Her mother shot her a sharp look and then said, "Well, are you ready? Mary, Sarah, and I have been waiting for some time." Her words came out as an accusation.

"*Jah*, I'm ready now." Rebecca, Sarah, and Mary exchanged glances. Mary shrugged one shoulder.

Soon, Mrs. Miller was driving the three women in the direction of the Yoders' farm. Betsy Yoder was Mrs. Miller's closest friend, but Rebecca did her best to avoid

Mrs. Yoder. She had a sharp tongue and did not mind giving her opinion on anything. She was possessed of a rather forceful personality.

David was outside the house, throwing sticks to Pirate. Beth Yoder was bending over something in the garden. She looked up and waved when she saw the buggy coming. Mary at once jumped down from the buggy and went over to David and their shared dog, Pirate, while Rebecca, Mrs. Miller, and Sarah walked over to Mrs. Yoder.

Mrs. Yoder clutched some peppermint leaves to her chest. "David spends a lot of time with that dog." There was a clear note of disapproval in her voice. "*Hiya*, Rebecca. *Hiya*, Sarah." She looked Sarah up and down.

Rebecca wondered if her mother and Mrs. Yoder would try to matchmake David with Sarah. She knew Mary liked David and she had often thought David liked Mary, but nothing had ever come of it.

"Come inside. We'll have some meadow tea." She waved the peppermint leaves at them. "I made some an hour ago and was going to make more. I asked my daughter, Jessie, to fetch the leaves, but she seems to have wandered away."

Rebecca looked over her shoulder at Mary and David with Pirate. She noted that the two of them were laughing together. *Maybe they are just good friends, after all*, Rebecca thought.

Beth indicated Rebecca and Sarah should sit while she and Mrs. Miller went into the kitchen. They returned presently and set a plate of chocolate whoopie pies and steaming mugs of meadow tea in front of the girls.

"So, what do you think of David?" Mrs. Yoder asked Sarah.

Sarah appeared horrified to be put on the spot. "Oh, um, he seems nice," she sputtered and then looked around the room wildly as if for inspiration.

Mrs. Yoder frowned deeply. To Mrs. Miller, she said, "I had hoped that David and Mary would marry. At first I didn't like the girl, if I am to be honest. She chatters away mindlessly at times." Beth broke off and stroked her chin. "However, I have become quite fond of her. She has a wide knowledge of cat health."

Rebecca thought her ears had deceived her. "Excuse me, did you say cat health?"

Mrs. Miller shot her a glare for daring to interrupt Mrs. Yoder.

Mrs. Yoder nodded solemnly. "*Jah*, that is right. Cat health. She has been a great help to me with my cats. I have several," she added rather unnecessarily. Rebecca had counted five cats so far and she figured there were more in other rooms. Right now she could see a fluffy cat perched atop a spare chair, a sleek black cat asleep under the dining table, two other cats playing, and one cat asleep in front of the fire.

"I have given up trying to match the girl with anyone," Mrs. Miller lamented, throwing both hands in the air in a dramatic gesture. "I was hoping someone new would come to the community. And then of course we need to find a husband for Sarah."

Sarah looked horror-stricken. Her hands flew to her throat. "Me?" she squeaked.

Rebecca was a little surprised at Sarah's reaction.

All the Miller girls had warned Sarah that their mother was an avid matchmaker, and Rebecca thought Sarah had believed them at the time. Maybe she had thought they were exaggerating. *Oh well, she will find out for herself soon enough*, Rebecca thought. She allowed herself a little chuckle.

"Oh, what shall I do with her?" Mrs. Miller continued.

Rebecca was glad they had not started on her. Maybe they just assumed she would be marrying Elijah.

"Sarah, you didn't actually tell me what you thought of David?" Mrs. Yoder persisted.

"Oh, he seems nice," Sarah said, and then bit her lip.

Mrs. Miller and Mrs. Yoder exchanged glances. *Could they be any more obvious?* Rebecca thought.

Mrs. Miller leaned across to Mrs. Yoder. "We had an *interesting* guest at dinner last night."

Beth Yoder was clearly intrigued. "Do tell. Who was it?"

"Samuel and Ida Flickinger's son, Eli. He arrived in town only yesterday."

"Maybe he will be a suitable match for Sarah or Mary."

Mrs. Miller laughed heartily. "*Nee, nee, nee*. He's English now. He calls himself Nash." Beth Yoder looked disappointed. Mrs. Miller pushed on. "And that's not all." She lowered her tone. "He has tattoos and a ring through his nose."

Beth Yoder's mouth fell open. She was rendered speechless for some time. After a long interval, she said, "He does?"

Mrs. Miller smiled and nodded. "And there's more," she said. "He is very rude and speaks his mind. He appears careless of the feelings of others."

"I wonder how I could meet him?" Beth Yoder said.

Mrs. Miller continued in the same conspiratorial tone. "The bishop visited with us yesterday and told me Eli Flickinger had arrived in town, but he didn't tell me he was English or mention his manner. I told the bishop I would invite the Flickingers for dinner. He said he was on his way to the B&B and would invite them for me."

"Ouch," Beth Yoder said as one of the cats jumped on her and startled her. "You will need to learn to retract your claws," Beth scolded the cat. She picked it up and deposited it gently on the ground. To Mrs. Miller, she said, "Then clearly, the bishop had not yet met him, or surely he would have warned you."

Mrs. Miller had a faraway look in her eyes. "Maybe he did, maybe he didn't. I can't be sure."

Just then, Mary came inside with David.

Mrs. Yoder greeted her warmly. "Mary, would you go to the kitchen and fetch some meadow tea for yourself and David?"

"*Jah*." Mary disappeared in the direction of the kitchen.

Rebecca considered that Beth Yoder and Mary certainly seemed to have a comfortable relationship now. It was a shame that David wasn't interested in Mary, because it seemed a suitable match.

When Mary returned, Mrs. Yoder asked her, "So, what do you think of Eli Flickinger?"

Before she had a chance to respond, David asked, "Who is Eli Flickinger?"

It was Mrs. Miller who answered. "The Flickingers' *sohn* arrived in town yesterday. He is staying with his parents at the B&B."

"What's he like?" David asked. Rebecca couldn't be sure, but she thought she noticed jealousy in his tone.

"Oh, he's very rude," Mary said curtly. "He's not very nice. He says what he thinks, and he was rude to Mr. and Mrs. Miller."

Beth looked at Mrs. Miller. "He was rude to you?"

"I'm not one to complain," Mrs. Miller said, "but yes, he's not the most pleasant young man I have ever encountered."

Beth stood up. "Rachel, would you help me in the kitchen?"

The two walked to the kitchen, their heads together. Rebecca knew that Mrs. Miller was going to tell Mrs. Yoder in private about everything that had happened.

"You said he was rude?" David prompted Mary. "What does he look like?"

Mary shrugged, but Rebecca responded. "He's English," Rebecca told him. "He has tattoos and a big ring in his nose. I've encountered him several times at the B&B and he is quite rude."

"In what way?" David asked, scratching his head.

"He's not tactful at all and he made his mother cry." Rebecca's hand flew to her mouth. She realized she had said too much.

"I'd never met anyone so rude," Mary continued.

"He was even ruder than you were when I first met you, David."

David frowned. "So, what does he look like?" he asked again.

"He's tall with black hair and dark eyes. He's handsome," Mary said with a giggle.

David's frown deepened and his jaw set hard.

I do believe David might be jealous, Rebecca thought. Yet if David and Mary liked each other, why had nothing happened between them after all this time?

Later that night, Mary and Rebecca were playing Scrabble on the floor in front of the fire. Sarah had already gone to bed, and Rebecca would have liked to retire also, but Mary was keen to keep playing. It was unlike Mary to stay up so late—usually she went to the *grossmammi haus* not long after dinner.

It was raining heavily, and on occasion the thunder shook the house ever so slightly.

Rebecca wondered why Mary was not going back to her own house. Finally, she said, "Mary, don't you have enough wood for your fire?"

Mary looked up at her, puzzled. "*Jah*, I have plenty of wood for my fire."

"Do you not want to get wet going back to your *haus*?"

"*Nee*, I don't mind a little bit of rain."

Rebecca stifled a yawn. "Then is there something on your mind?"

"What makes you think I have something on my mind?" Mary countered.

"Because you don't usually stay up so late and I get the feeling you want to talk to me."

Mary let out a long sigh and leaned backward. "You're right. I just don't know how to bring up the subject."

"Just say it," Rebecca said. "You'll feel better once you do."

"It's about David Yoder."

"You already told me you like him," Rebecca said.

Mary nodded slowly. "*Jah. Jah*, I do. I can't understand it. He doesn't seem interested in any other girls, but he has never once asked me on a buggy ride. Yet I always feel like he really does like me."

"I don't want to get your hopes up, but I do think he likes you too," Rebecca admitted.

"I wanted to ask you if you thought he seemed interested in me today at his house."

"I did. I think he was jealous when his mother mentioned Nash Grayson."

Mary beamed. Rebecca waved one hand at her. "But I'm no expert on love, that's for sure! I'm the only one of my sisters who is left unmarried."

"You're the youngest," Mary pointed out.

Rebecca shrugged. She stood up and poked the fire, and then put another log on it. "It's going to be a bad winter this year," she said.

"Stop changing the subject, Rebecca. What will I do?"

Rebecca sat down again. She always found fires relaxing and the smell of wood comforting. "I don't know," she said. "Maybe you could ask one of my *schweschders* for their advice. They're all married."

"I asked Martha some time ago and she thought David liked me too. She was just as mystified as I was. And when Gary brings Sam to the Yoders' *haus* to play with Pirate, David seems awfully jealous. Even Gary told me he thought David was jealous."

"And Gary has never taken Laura to the Yoders' to play with Pirate?"

Mary smiled. "*Nee*, Laura is always working, so David doesn't know about her."

Rebecca shot Mary a sharp look. "Are you trying to make David jealous?"

Mary shrugged one shoulder. "Well, yes! But what good has it done?"

Rebecca thought on it some more. "Maybe he likes you, but he doesn't think you like him."

"Gary is bringing Sam to play with Pirate tomorrow afternoon," Mary said. "Rebecca, would you please come with me and tell me what you think? It will be after you finish work for the day."

Rebecca pondered it for a moment. "I suppose so, but surely you must have some indication how David feels about you?"

"I don't know," Mary said. "I often think he likes me, but it's been so long now. Anyone else would have asked me on a buggy ride ages and ages ago."

"I wish we could find out," Rebecca said. "What a shame you're not friends with his *schweschder*, Jessie."

Mary pulled a face. "I don't think Jessie has any

friends. She seems quite mean-spirited, and she's always trying to cause trouble."

"She did her best to stop Jacob and Esther getting together," Rebecca said. "Do you know, when you were out of the room, Mrs. Yoder said she was fond of you, and she had hoped you and David would get together."

Mary jumped to her feet. "*Wunderbar*! Why didn't you tell me that before?"

"I only just remembered. Anyways, I don't want to upset you, but she seems to have given up on you and David getting together too. I'm sorry, Mary."

Mary's face fell. "I suppose I should be happy at least that Mrs. Yoder likes me." She sighed once more. "I am sure I will never be married. And what about you, Rebecca? Do you think you will ever be married?"

Rebecca pulled a face, and the two girls sat there staring into the fire until the thunderstorm passed.

Chapter Seven

Rebecca was nervous accompanying Mary to the Yoders' *haus* that afternoon. She knew Mary would ask her many questions when they returned home, and she didn't want to get it wrong and mislead Mary. For a long time Rebecca had thought that David was interested in Mary, but he had done nothing about it. He wasn't overly shy, so she didn't understand why.

In fact, she had discussed it with Martha some months ago and Martha's opinion was that perhaps David was embarrassed about his past. After all, he had dated English girls when on *rumspringa*, whereas Mary was so sweet and virtuous. Rebecca, in fact, wondered if that was the case. Rebecca also wondered if Jessie Yoder had done something to keep the two apart, but when she had suggested that to Mary, Mary had said that could not be the case at all. Mary said she very rarely saw Jessie Yoder.

As Rebecca drove the buggy toward the Yoders' *haus*, Mary said, "Oh no!"

"Whatever is wrong?" Rebecca asked her.

"Gary is here already!"

Rebecca was puzzled. "But why does that matter?"

"Gary feels quite uncomfortable around David. He said David makes him tense, and that's why I always get here early. It seems Gary might be a little early today."

They got out of the buggy. Sam was throwing sticks for Pirate to fetch. Rebecca had heard that Sam had stopped twirling sticks but still collected rocks. Gary had reported to Mary who had reported to Rebecca that Sam was quite obsessed with his toy train set. However, he kept his toy trains at home.

As Rebecca and Mary walked over to the group, Mary elbowed Rebecca in the ribs. "Stay sharp!" she said. "You have to keep an eye on David and you have to tell me what you think later."

"*Jah*, I will," Rebecca said warily. *What if get it wrong?* she silently asked herself for the umpteenth time.

Rebecca stared at David. He certainly didn't seem to be relaxed. His arms were crossed over his chest and his expression was somber. "*Hiya*, Rebecca," he said in a lifeless manner, followed in a slightly more animated fashion by, "*Hiya*, Mary."

Mary went over to Sam and he handed her a stick to throw to Pirate. Rebecca stood by the herb garden with Gary and David. "How is Sam going?" Rebecca asked Gary. "Martha asks after him all the time."

"We're getting him a dog. A pet dog," Gary said. "A Labrador, in fact."

Rebecca was pleased. "Sam will love that. Are you

getting him a service dog?" Rebecca knew there was one service dog in their community. Matthew Lehman had a service dog to help alert him to his high or low blood sugar for his diabetes.

"No, Sam doesn't really need a service dog," Gary said. "Martha told me you know a service dog. Does he help someone with diabetes?"

"Yes, as a matter of fact," Rebecca said. "He's a Staffordshire Terrier."

"Service dogs are good for people who have problems with mobility or perhaps a hearing or visual impairments or even epilepsy," Gary added.

"So you don't have service dogs for children on the autism spectrum?"

Gary shrugged. "Yes some do, but his therapist said just a pet dog would be fine for him."

"Not a therapy dog?" Rebecca asked. "When I was in the hospital, a therapy dog was often brought around. She was a Golden Retriever. Even the dentist has a therapy dog."

"Yes, children on the autism spectrum can have therapy dogs, service dogs, or companion dogs, but Sam's autism therapist said the companion dog would be good for him."

"Have you found a suitable dog for him yet?" Rebecca asked him.

Gary nodded. "Yes, and Sam's thrilled. The dog arrives this week."

"Has he met the dog?"

"Oh yes, several times, both with his autism therapist and without."

Gary made to walk over to Mary, Sam, and Pirate, but David prevented him. He stepped in front of him ever so slightly. "They're having fun by themselves."

Gary appeared to be at a loss. "Um, err yes," he sputtered. He looked at Rebecca and raised his eyebrows.

Rebecca had no idea how to respond so simply smiled and nodded. "*Jah*, they're having a good time together," she said.

"The three of them are such good friends," Gary said. "Sam is very fond of Mary."

"Mary will have her own *kinner* one day," David said with narrowed eyes. His cheeks burned beet red and a dark look covered his face.

Surely, David must have some interest in Mary to react like this, Rebecca thought. *Mary will ask me what I think, so I have to try to remember all the little details.* As soon as she thought that, she was worried that she would forget. Rebecca frowned in concentration.

Gary usually came on the days when Mrs. Yoder was in town. Rebecca had long thought that was deliberate, so it was with some horror she saw Mrs. Yoder's buggy coming up the road at a fast pace. Mrs. Yoder nodded to the group and drove her horse straight past them and over to the barn.

Some time later, Mrs. Yoder walked over to where Rebecca, David, and Gary were still watching Mary and Sam play with Pirate.

"*Hullo*, Gary," she said with narrowed eyes.

"Hello, Mrs. Yoder," Gary said. He was clearly quite discomforted.

Rebecca wondered how often the two had met.

"I haven't seen you for some months," Mrs. Yoder continued.

Gary smiled and nodded.

Well then, that answers my question, Rebecca thought.

"Why don't the three of you sit on the porch and I'll fetch some lemonade?"

They thanked Mrs. Yoder. David was first onto the porch. The three of them sat in uncomfortable silence until Mrs. Yoder returned with tall glasses of lemonade on a tray. She handed a glass to each person and then directly addressed Gary. "How is your mother?"

"She's well, thank you," Gary said.

"And how is your wife?"

Gary looked shocked. "But, um, I don't have a wife," Gary stammered.

"Surely you have a girlfriend?"

Gary bit his lip and stared at the ground. Rebecca had never asked Mary outright, but she assumed Mary had told Gary to pretend he didn't have a girlfriend to help make David jealous. Whatever the case, Gary now answered honestly. "Yes, I do have a girlfriend, Laura."

Mrs. Yoder shot David a look and disappeared inside.

David cleared his throat and fidgeted. Rebecca wondered if David had actually discussed his feelings for Mary with his mother, or whether Mrs. Yoder was simply curious. She decided it was likely the latter.

Rebecca tried to think of something to say, so she could see how David felt about Mary.

"So David, you don't have a girlfriend, do you?" she asked him.

David was clearly alarmed to be asked such a question. "*Nee*!" he exclaimed in a high-pitched voice. He looked like a startled deer.

"Isn't that funny. Mary doesn't have a boyfriend either."

David frowned. "Are you sure?" He fixed Rebecca with a steely gaze.

"Yes, of course she doesn't." Rebecca filed that conversation away to report to Mary. David seemed to think Mary had a boyfriend, but that was a strange thing to think. Surely David couldn't possibly think Mary was dating someone. David and Mary both attended the same meetings; they both attended the same Singings. This was a small community and everyone knew what everyone else was doing. If Mary had a boyfriend, then everyone would know.

Just then Jessie Yoder walked around the building. She stopped short when she saw the three of them, and scowled. "Rebecca," she snapped. "I thought only Mary was here. I didn't know you were here. *Hullo*, Gary."

"Hello, Jessie," he said easily. Rebecca considered Gary did not seem at all intimidated by Jessie whereas he was noticeably quite intimidated by David and Mrs. Yoder. "What are you doing, Jessie?"

"I've been smoking behind the barn so my mother won't catch me," she said.

Gary laughed and slammed his hand on his leg, but Rebecca knew Jessie wasn't joking. David shifted once more in his hickory chair.

Jessie walked inside without so much as a backward glance.

"Awkward!" Gary said. "Your sister is not like the rest of you."

David simply raised his eyebrows and did not respond.

Mary walked over, holding Sam's hand. "Sam's very excited. He told me you're collecting his dog next week."

"And he's a very nice dog too."

"Yes, Sam's beside himself with excitement," Mary said.

Sam, in fact, was beaming.

"Does that mean you won't bring him back to see Pirate anymore?" David said, glaring at Gary.

"Of course Sam will keep seeing Pirate," Mary said, frowning at David. "Do you still want to see Pirate after you get your own dog, Sam?"

Sam nodded vigorously and patted the Pirate's head.

Mary folded her arms over her chest. "Why would you say such a thing, David? You might have upset him."

"I didn't mean to upset him," David said in chastened tones.

Gary patted David hard on the back. "It's all right. You didn't mean to upset him."

Rebecca considered she was in a most uncomfortable situation. The atmosphere was so tense. Mary and Sam were the only ones who seemed oblivious to the tension.

Mrs. Yoder must have heard Mary and Sam speaking, as she hurried out with another tray. "*Hullo* Sam, I haven't seen you for a long time, have I?"

Sam leaned into Mary and looked at the ground. Mrs.

Yoder handed him a glass of lemonade. "Why don't you come and sit on the porch and have some chocolate whoopie pies?"

Sam hurried up the stairs and sat down. Mary sat next to him and Mrs. Yoder placed the plate of whoopie pies between them. Sam chatted away to Mary about his new dog.

"Mary will make a great mother some day," Gary said to no one in particular.

"But you have a girlfriend," David snapped.

Gary did not respond, but simply scratched his head, looked at Rebecca, and raised his eyebrows.

Rebecca shrugged one shoulder.

David was indeed acting jealous, but if he liked Mary, then what was stopping him? Something certainly was. Rebecca had a momentary urge to ask to speak to David alone and ask him outright. She realized that she couldn't do that unless Mary specifically asked her to do so.

Later, as Rebecca and Mary were driving away from the Yoders' house, Mary turned to Rebecca. "I can't wait to hear what you think. Do you think he likes me? Or do you think he doesn't? You can tell me—I won't be upset. Well, of course I'll be upset, but I still want you to tell me anyway. I'd rather know whether it's good or bad. You can be quite blunt. Please don't think you have to spare my feelings. Even if I'm devastated and sad, it's better that I know the truth. Yes, I really want to know the truth. Please tell me, Rebecca."

Rebecca waited for Mary to pause for breath, and

then took the opportunity to speak. "This is my honest opinion. I don't want to be wrong and get your hopes up though, but it really seems to me that David likes you."

Mary clasped her hands in delight.

"But the bad news is," Rebecca continued, "that he hasn't done anything about it. So then, there has to be a reason. Would you like me to ask him what it is?"

Mary clutched her throat in alarm. "*Nee*, *nee*, *nee*!" She took a deep breath and then added, "It's very nice of you to offer, but no, I would be absolutely mortified! So tell me everything he said, right from the beginning."

Rebecca tried to remember everything that was said and repeated it word for word to Mary. Mary was silent for a long while, so Rebecca finally said, "Mary, are you all right? You haven't said anything."

"Like you said, there must be a reason why he hasn't asked me on a date. Maybe it's because he thinks I have a boyfriend."

"But that doesn't make any sense, because if you had a boyfriend, then the whole community would know about it," Rebecca pointed out.

Mary thought some more and then added, "*Jah*, I'd say he probably said that because he was trying to figure out if I was interested in a boy in the community."

Rebecca nodded. "Yes, that makes sense," she agreed.

By the time they reached the Millers' house, Rebecca had a sore throat from repeating what David had said over and over again. Still, Mary was not satisfied, and Rebecca's heart went out to her. It was clear to her that Mary was head over heels in love with David, and if she had to hazard a guess, she would say that David was very fond of Mary, at the very least. It was also just as clear that something was stopping him from asking Rebecca on a date, but Rebecca could not figure out what that something was.

Chapter Eight

On this particular Monday, the Miller *haus* was a hive of activity; not one person, even a child, was standing still or not fully engaged in a chore. As an Amish wedding was one of the rare occasions on which the husbands helped their *fraas* in the kitchen, there was standing room only, as was usual the day before such an occasion. It was busy, but there was order. Food was everywhere: all manner of puddings, cracker pudding, caramel pudding, vanilla cornstarch pudding, date pudding, bread pudding, rice pudding, banana pudding; every type of whoopie pie imaginable, and mountains of potatoes were being peeled for the mashed potatoes, all to be served the following day. Two women were chopping tomatoes and cucumbers, while another two women were shredding lettuce.

One person was making plates of haystacks to hand out to the hungry masses who were helping: piles of rice and crushed crackers, on a base of lettuce, and topped with cooked hamburger and chopped vegetables, with cheese on top. There was no time to stop to eat; people ate while they worked, and at all different times.

Martha hurried out once more to the mobile kitchen the Millers had rented for the wedding. Renting a mobile kitchen was a necessity for weddings in the community, for while the people were used to hosting large numbers every second Sunday for church meetings, more than double or even triple that number would attend a wedding, as weddings invariably attracted large numbers of relatives from out of town.

One end of the large commercial kitchen held both a walk-in refrigerator and a walk-in freezer. The rest of the trailer was lined with stainless steel preparation areas on one side, and on the other, a commercial oven, and all manner of deep fryers, shallow fryers, grills, griddles, and sinks on the other side. The sinks even had their own purposes: hand washing, pot washing, and vegetable washing.

The mobile kitchen came with two 750 watt generators for use if necessary, but as Mr. Miller had permission from the bishop to use electricity in his barn, which was his place of business for furniture making, the trailer simply connected to that power supply. It did, however, have over two hundred pounds of propane for the commercial oven. The mobile kitchen contained cutlery, crockery, pans, and everything needed for wedding preparation.

Mrs. Flickinger was sitting in the kitchen at the large, oak table with Rebecca making pastry. There was so much need for pastry: apple pies, sugar cream pies, butterscotch pies, pumpkin pies, shoestring apple pies, as well as pastry for fry pies containing apples, cherries, blueberries, and peaches.

The bishop's wife, Fannie Graber, who was known far and wide for her unusual food combinations, was making chocolate flakey pastry for her potato and tuna pies.

Martha was making layered desserts with pineapple and peaches alternating with green and red Jell-O.

Mrs. Flickinger nodded to Martha. "You and Moses must come and see our *haus*."

"I'd love to, *denki*. I haven't seen inside it since I was little. Rebecca tells me you've done wonders with it, converting it to a B&B."

Mrs. Flickinger beamed. "We were blessed to find such a *haus* when we moved here. The early Mennonite architecture suits a B&B and the guests are fascinated by the built-in German Bible closets and the deep windowsills. The whole dining and kitchen area has the early corner cupboards with the bubble glass and the keystone hinges."

Rebecca looked up from her pastry. "*Jah*, it's *wunderbar*."

Martha smiled and said, "Sounds it!" and then placed the layered desserts on a tray somewhat precariously. "I'll take these out to the refrigerator."

Sarah rushed over to Rebecca carrying a pot of melted chocolate. "Rebecca, hurry! Bring the graham crackers."

Rebecca looked at Sarah. "Why the hurry?"

Sarah's face was anxious. "Martha won't approve of

us making these cookies with plain, old, coating chocolate. We have to get them all done before she gets back."

Rebecca chuckled. "I know Martha has her chocolate business and is very particular about the chocolates she makes, but I'm sure that she won't mind us serving up these cookies." Rebecca took one look at Sarah's worried face and decided to humor her. After all, Martha and Sarah had become close friends. "Okay, I'll help you."

Sarah hurried over to Rebecca with peanut butter and a large quantity of melted chocolate. The girls soon had made many cookies by sandwiching peanut butter between two graham crackers, and then dipping it in melted chocolate. By the time Martha returned, there were numerous cookies drying and hardening on wax paper. "Why are you looking at me?" she asked as she walked back through the door.

"No reason." Rebecca walked over to Martha.

Martha simply shrugged. "Elijah's just arrived if you want to speak to him."

Sarah spoke before Rebecca could respond to Martha. "I just have to finish up here."

Rebecca stared at Sarah. *Why would Martha be speaking to Sarah about Elijah?* she wondered. Her uneasiness grew as Sarah soon hurried outside, presumably to speak to Elijah.

"Martha, were you speaking to Sarah or to me about Elijah?"

Martha looked up, puzzled. "Why, to you, of course." When Rebecca didn't answer, Martha continued, "You'll be next, Rebecca."

"Next for what?" Rebecca's reply brought laughter from everyone present.

"To marry of course."

"Oh." Rebecca didn't know what to say, and was suddenly perturbed as everyone in the kitchen was looking at her.

Mrs. Weaver, a kindly, elderly widow, took her arm. "Isn't that lovely, dear. Your three *schweschders* are married to the three Hostetler *bruders*, and when you marry Elijah Hostetler, that will make it complete."

"But I'm not marrying Elijah," Rebecca protested.

"That's right, dear," the hard-of-hearing Mrs. Weaver said. "Your wedding will be next. I hope your *mudder* has many chickens being fattened in readiness for your wedding. Oh how happy your *mudder* must be, and Elijah's *mudder* too. Soon you and Elijah will have plenty of *bopplin*."

The people in the room chuckled at some length, most likely driven on by Rebecca's horrified expression. "I'm not marrying Elijah," Rebecca insisted as loudly as she could.

Mrs. Weaver looked upset. "Don't worry, dear. Go and speak to the bishop and he'll be able to help you two with your problems."

There's no point saying any more, Rebecca thought. She picked up a large tray of apple pies. "I'll just take these out the refrigerator in the mobile kitchen," she announced.

On her way to the mobile kitchen, Rebecca walked past Elijah and Sarah, who stopped speaking as soon as she approached. The three smiled at each other and

Rebecca kept going. *Why did they stop talking as soon as they saw me?* she wondered. *I hope they're not dating.* Tears pricked at Rebecca's eyes. Despite her protestations, she did want to marry Elijah, but not just yet. Everyone expected them to marry, and Rebecca wanted to make very sure that Elijah really wanted to marry her for the sole reason that he was truly in love with her, not just because it was something that was expected by the whole community.

Rebecca loved Elijah with her whole heart; she had loved him for as long as she could remember. The only trouble was, she had no idea how Elijah felt about her. He was her best friend, and they usually teased each other and joked with each other.

Rebecca had always felt that she would marry Elijah one day, but had never felt any urgency about that matter—at least, not until now.

Rebecca carefully placed the apple pies in the walk-in refrigerator, and then hurried back out the door, straight into the hard chest of a young man.

"Sorry," she said automatically, before she looked and saw that the person was none other than Nash Grayson. She recoiled, a fact that did not go unnoticed by Nash. "Sorry, Nash, *err*, Eli, *err*, Nash." Rebecca had no idea how to address the young *mann*, and fumbled with her apron in an attempt to hide her awkwardness.

Nash was visibly annoyed. "It's Nash," he said, with irritation in his voice.

"Nash," Rebecca repeated. "What are you doing here?"

"Helping, obviously. *Englischers* aren't forbidden to help the day before a wedding, are they."

"I don't know," Rebecca said, and then put her hand to her mouth when she realized it was said as a statement and not a question, and at that, with more than a little bit of sarcasm. She wished she would learn to think before she spoke. "Of course not. *Um*, it's *gut* that you're helping."

Rebecca looked up to see that Elijah was studying her carefully. Sarah was still speaking to him in an animated fashion, but he was staring at Rebecca. A little thrill of excitement ran through Rebecca as she wondered if Elijah was jealous.

Nash Grayson was no fool; he had seen Elijah watching him and Rebecca. *So, I have competition*, he thought. Still, that blonde girl, Sarah, was talking to Elijah. If he could help get those two together, that would leave the way clear for him and Rebecca. It was simple: all he had to do was to drive a wedge between Rebecca and Elijah and find a way to get Sarah and Elijah together.

So that's Nash Grayson, Elijah thought. *I suppose girls might find him handsome. He's tall, and he looks mysterious. I believe girls like that sort of thing.*

Elijah was uncomfortable over the cozy conversation that Nash and Rebecca appeared to be having. He had come to ask Rebecca on a buggy ride, but had been waylaid by Sarah asking him all sorts of questions about his *mudder's* quilt store. Hannah had been taking in sewing for his *mudder* and doing it at her *haus*, but she was now overwhelmed with the twins and had told Katie Hostetler that she could no longer continue. It seemed that Sarah wanted to be her replacement.

Elijah had, however, been gratified that Rebecca had flashed him what he hoped was a look of jealously when she saw him speaking with Sarah. Perhaps Rebecca didn't find Nash all that attractive, after all. Elijah certainly hoped that was the case.

Chapter Nine

By dawn on the morning of Martha's wedding to Moses, Rebecca was already exhausted, not only by the hard work of the day before, for she was used to hard work, but by the constant jokes that she would be the next to be married, and at that, to Elijah. Sure, the jokes were well-meaning, but that did not in any way lessen their impact. One or two jokes might have been funny, but the constant barrage of them was tiring.

The wedding service began at 8 a.m., and there was still plenty to do. Mr. Miller had set up a tie-line for the horses, and many horses were already tethered there, with a long line of buggies parked in the nearby field. Their attendants, young teenage boys, were hurrying around efficiently, making sure that everything was in order.

Rebecca poked her head inside the mobile kitchen, looking for her *mudder*. Four couples were in there, preparing the *roascht*, the traditional Amish wedding roast of chickens and stuffing bread with spices and celery. A further four couples were mashing copious amounts of potatoes while a further two women were making sure that there would be an unending supply of freshly brewed *kaffi*.

There was no sign of Mrs. Miller, so Rebecca hurried back into the *haus* to consult the notes, which had been drawn up by Martha. She ran her finger down the list of cooks' names on one side, and the items that each person was cooking on the other. Everything appeared to be running smoothly.

Her *mudder* was there in the kitchen, making gravy. "*Mamm*, what would you like me to do now?" Rebecca asked. "The creamed celery's all done and so is the gravy."

Mrs. Miller looked up briefly. "*Gut*. You can go and start as a *Vorgeher* now."

The Old German word *Vorgeher* meant a leader, but in the context of Amish weddings it meant an usher. Elijah and Rebecca had both agreed to be ushers, a job often given to the siblings of both the bride and the groom. For the wedding ceremony, Martha had two *newehockers*, "side-sitters" or attendants, and so therefore did Moses. As Martha's *schweschders* were married to Moses' *bruders*, it was clear that the two couples would be the *newehockers*.

The traditional number of the *newehockers* was two for the bride and two for the groom, although in some communities in Lancaster, three *newehockers* each were becoming more frequent. Rebecca, however, did not want to be so closely thrown together with Elijah yet again, so had said she would rather be a *Vorgeher* than a *newehocker.* This had pleased her *mudder*, who had more of a traditional mindset. Mrs. Miller always said that any break in tradition was of the devil, not that she professed to believe in the existence of the devil apart from his literal existence as a Biblical entity, and of course, Mrs. Miller did firmly believe in hell. This paradox of their *mudder's* was one that the Miller girls had always wondered about, although were never impolite enough to ask.

Rebecca hurried outside to the community's bench wagon which had delivered the benches as well as all the folding chairs for the elderly guests. The folding chairs were also used for elderly folk at the church services. At any rate, it would be difficult for the elderly to sit through the three hours of the wedding service on backless benches. The bench wagon also contained the hymn books. It was Rebecca's duty to meet with the other ushers to confirm the layout of the tables and benches for the reception. They had already had a rehearsal of turning the benches into tables and seats for the reception the day before.

Rebecca's heart fluttered when she saw Elijah, who caught her eye and smiled. Rebecca walked over to speak to Elijah, but to her dismay, Sarah appeared, and handed Elijah a mug of *kaffi*. Rebecca's heart sank; the two of them already looked like a couple, and given the Amish fondness for secrecy when dating, they could already be a couple for all she knew.

Elijah thanked Sarah and looked at Rebecca expectantly, but she ducked into the large tent that stood against the wide open doors of the barn. The large tent provided extra seating, and was where the *Englischer* guests were to sit during the ceremony. Mrs. Hostetler, the *mudder* of the groom, as well as of Elijah, owned a quilt store and had made several *Englisch* friends, as had Mr. Miller in the course of his furniture making business.

Rebecca clutched at her stomach. Had she made a grave mistake in waiting for Elijah to show he did indeed love her with all his might? Or had the fact that she was waiting for him to declare his affections left the way open for another girl?

"Are you all right?"

Rebecca looked up at the owner of the voice to see Nash Grayson looming over her, his face full of concern.

"*Jah*, *denki*," she said.

"You've gone all white."

"Are you staying for the wedding?" Rebecca said by way of reply, mentally assessing where Nash should be seated. He would have to be seated with the *Englischers*, of course.

"No," he said. "I've just brought my mother here. Disappointed?"

Rebecca was puzzled. "What, disappointed that your *mudder* is here? What do you mean?"

Nash laughed so hard that he clutched his sides. "No, silly. Are you disappointed that I won't be here for the wedding?"

Rebecca was about to say something cutting, but saw that Elijah had stuck his head inside the tent and was watching them. She felt it only proper to introduce the two *menner.* “Nash, this is Elijah Hostetler, the *bruder* of the groom. Elijah, this is…”

Nash cut her off. “Hi, I’m Nash Grayson.” He put out his hand and Elijah shook it. “I’m staying at the B&B for some time. I just gave Mrs. Flickinger, the owner of the B&B, a ride here in my car. I’m leaving now.”

Aha, so he doesn’t want anyone to know that he’s really Eli Flickinger, Rebecca thought.

Nash nodded to Elijah, winked at Rebecca, and then left. By the look on Elijah’s face, it was clear that he had seen the wink. Rebecca struggled with her loyalties. Should she tell Elijah the truth about Nash, when it was clear that Nash had tried to keep the truth from him? If she didn’t, the truth would soon get out, and Elijah would wonder why Rebecca hadn’t told him. That secret was not one that would last for any length of time in the community. Nash had put Rebecca in a difficult position, a difficult position indeed.

Why didn’t Rebecca tell me that Nash Grayson was the Flickingers’ son? Elijah wondered. *She would have no idea that I already know, so it’s not gut that she’s keeping secrets from me. It’s obvious that Nash didn’t want me to know his true identity. Besides, that Nash has a nerve, winking at Rebecca like that.*

Had Elijah being so slow to ask Rebecca to marry him left the way open for her to have feelings for another *mann*? He had been looking for an opportunity to speak with Rebecca, but Sarah had stuck to him like glue, asking all sorts of questions about his *mudder’s* store. He had finally told her that she needed to speak to his *mudder*.

He had enjoyed the proximity to Rebecca that day, despite all the jokes that came his way about him being the last Hostetler *bruder* to marry the last Miller *schweschder*. If he'd heard that joke once, he'd heard it a thousand times. It became wearying after a while.

His heart belonged to Rebecca; of that he was certain. Yet he had no idea how she felt about him. Did she too feel the pressure to marry him? If he proposed to her, would she marry him only because it was expected of her? Elijah wanted true love, the sort that his *bruders* had. Was he silly to want that? Or should he propose to Rebecca and be grateful if she agreed to marry him, even if she didn't love him and thought of him only as a *gut* friend?

Chapter Ten

As would be expected with every Amish wedding preparation, the morning had run smoothly and to plan. Rebecca and Elijah had shown the guests to their seats, and everyone was now seated in the correct, traditional order.

Rebecca finally sat down, relieved and excited that Martha was about to be married. Just on 8 a.m., everyone started singing the first traditional wedding hymn in German. The ministers walked out the barn, followed by Martha and Moses. While Rebecca was singing the hymn which was about the church as Christ's bride, she stole a look at Martha. Martha and her two *newehockers*, Hannah and Esther, were all wearing the same purple dresses, along with their aprons and prayer *kapps*. Martha was wearing black, high-topped boots. Moses and his two *newehockers*, Noah and Jacob, were wearing black suits, black brimmed hats, white shirts, and black high-topped boots. Moses was wearing a black hat with a wide brim. Rebecca thought that Martha looked nervous, and even the ever-cheerful Moses looked solemn. This was Martha and Moses' time of *Abroth*, the questions that the bishop would ask them, and then the advice he would give them.

The next song was *Das Loblied*, "The Song of Praise," from the Amish hymn book, the *Ausbund*. Rebecca smiled to herself while singing the hymn in the traditional, very slow manner. *Mamm will be happy that this wedding is traditional*, she thought, *not that Martha had any choice in the matter. I wonder if anyone from the community will ever break away from tradition in their wedding?*

Rebecca had a momentary pang of guilt for thinking such thoughts, and then her thoughts turned to her own wedding. *It will be right here, just like this wedding*, she thought, but then suddenly felt downcast. *What if I never get married? I won't marry Elijah unless he's truly in love with me, but he's never shown any sign that he is. I'm sure he just expects to marry me—me, the last Miller girl, marrying the last Hostetler boy. All my schweschders are married to his bruders, and the whole community expects us to marry. I think Elijah is just falling into everyone's expectations for us.*

Rebecca fell deeper into sadness for her future, when, after around fifteen minutes of singing *Das Loblied*, Martha and Moses reappeared, and this cheered her up. Martha and Moses went to sit next to their *newehockers*, who were sitting on the benches in front of the ministers. Moses took up his position on the bench next to his *newehockers*, his *bruders* Noah and Jacob. The three of them were on the bench directly opposite the bench on which Martha, and her attendants, her *schweschders* Hannah and Esther, were sitting.

Rebecca wondered again what it would be like to marry Elijah. *If I married Elijah, I'd have to have all three of my schweschders as newehockers*, she thought. *Then Mamm would be really annoyed with me for breaking tradition.* She suppressed a chuckle.

Rebecca turned her attention back to singing, as the third hymn had begun. Like the first hymn, this hymn was also about the church as the bride of Christ.

One of the ministers then stood up and launched into a talk about marriage in the Old Testament. Two hours later, everyone present kneeled for a silent prayer, and then stood up when Matthew chapter nineteen, verses one through twelve were read out loud.

The bishop then started his talk, beginning in Genesis. Rebecca shifted her weight on the bench and looked in the direction of Elijah. Would she one day marry Elijah? She loved him with all her heart, but did he love her back? She did not want to spend her lifetime in a loveless marriage. Sure, Elijah would make a wonderful husband, but she wanted more. She wanted his love. Elijah was kind-hearted and sweet, and everyone expected the two of them to marry. *He probably thinks it's his duty to marry me*, she thought with dismay. The pressure on the two of them to marry had been considerable. Sure, it was always said in a joking, light hearted manner, but it was there, nonetheless. With her three older *schweschders* married to his three older *bruders*, most people considered it a done deal that Rebecca would marry Elijah.

Rebecca was away with her thoughts of marriage and Elijah when she heard the bishop say, "Now here are two in one faith." This meant that he had come to the end of his talk and was starting the short, actual marriage ceremony. The bishop continued by asking the assembly if anyone knew of any reason why Martha and Moses could not be married. The bishop paused so long that Rebecca nearly had a fit of the giggles. She remembered this part of Esther and Jacob's wedding, when she had imagined that Jessie Yoder would run to the bishop with a fanciful story.

The bishop finally spoke again. "If it is still your desire to be married, you might in the name of the Lord come forth." He told Moses and Martha to stand in front of him.

The bishop then questioned Moses and Martha in turn. "Moses, do you believe and confess with your mouth that it is scriptural order for one man and one woman to be one, and state that you have been thus led so far?" After Moses affirmed, he repeated the same question to Martha. The bishop turned back to Moses. "Moses, can you, *bruder*, state that the Lord directs you to take this *schweschder* as your wife?" The bishop then addressed the question to Martha.

The bishop continued to question Moses. "Moses, do you promise to support your *fraa* when she is in weakness, sickness, whatever trials might befall you, and stand as a Christian husband?" Again, the parallel question was put to Martha.

The final question put to Moses and Martha was, "Do you vow to remain together, and have love, consideration, and forbearance one for another and not to part from one another until beloved *Gott* shall finally part you in death?"

The bishop now picked up the German prayer book known as the *Die Ernsthafte Christenpflicht*, "Prayer Book for Earnest Christians." This book was first printed in 1708, and Rebecca knew it well, as did the rest of the community. He read aloud, "The Prayer for Those About to Be Married."

The bishop then read from the *Book of Tobit*. Rebecca had found out only recently that Amish, Mennonites, and Catholics approved of the *Book of Tobit*, but that other Christians did not consider it canon. Martha had told her, as Martha had lived for a short time with *Englischers*. The bishop read from *The Book of Tobit,* chapter seven, verse fifteen. "And taking the right hand of his daughter, Raguel gave it unto the right hand of Tobias, and saith, 'The *Gott* of Abraham, the *Gott* of Isaac, the *Gott* of Jacob be with you, and might He join you together, and fulfill His blessing in you.'"

The bishop now came to the last words of the actual marriage ceremony. "Go ye forth in the name of the Lord. Ye are now *mann* and *fraa*."

The actual marriage ceremony had taken about four minutes and had come at the end of three hours of talks by the ministers and the bishop. Martha and Moses returned to their seats in the front row. Rebecca stifled another giggle as she thought of *Englisch* weddings where the bride and groom kiss in front of everyone. She was glad she did not giggle, for not a sound could be heard; one could hear a pin drop. Silence always prevailed at such occasions.

Everyone then turned around to kneel in front of the benches for the long, silent prayer, which marked the end of the wedding service.

Rebecca's thoughts drifted away once again to Elijah. Would he one day marry her? Would the two of them one day stand in front of the bishop in this very barn? How would she ever know Elijah's true feelings for her?

On the one hand, Elijah was happy that his *bruder* Moses was now married to his true love, Martha, but on the other hand he was a little sad that Rebecca might not love him. He had thought of Rebecca throughout the entire service, and had decided that he would ask her to marry him. He would rather be married to Rebecca, even if she was only marrying him out of duty. Surely her love for him would grow; surely Rebecca would come to love him.

As the guests filed out of the barn, Rebecca hurried to help prepare for the first sitting of the meal, nodding a hurried greeting to the *Ecktender*, wedding-corner attendants, who were likewise hurrying. The *Ecktenders* were her *onkels* and *aentis*. While some couples in the community now had the wedding party's dining table in the center of the room, there was no way that Mrs. Miller would tolerate what she called such a blatant and deplorable break from tradition, so this wedding party would be seated in the traditional *Eck*, the corner, of the room. In the *Eck*, two long rows of benches and tables met at a right angle.

Rebecca joined Elijah in supervising the setting up of the benches and the tables for the meals to come. The meals would be served in shifts given the few hundred people present. Elijah suddenly smiled at Rebecca, which set her stomach off into flutters. Rebecca felt slightly nauseous and allowed herself a brief moment to wonder how being in love could make someone feel physically sick.

It took three of the church benches to make up one table. Elijah, guided by the careful chalk marks of the previous day, helped Rebecca slip the legs of the benches into the plywood trusses, his shoulder momentarily brushing hers as he did so. This set off tingles coursing through Rebecca, right down to her toes. She sighed aloud.

Elijah looked at her with concern and she nodded to say she was all right. She loved the way they could communicate without words. In fact, there were many things she loved about Elijah; if only he felt the same way.

Now that the three benches were flat and parallel with each other, and at table height, Elijah then clamped them into place. He and Rebecca then hurried away in different directions to make sure that all tables were now set up, and they directed the people who had agreed to help the ushers to place all tables in the prearranged spots. Now the only job that remained was to place the remaining benches at each table and to place a white cloth on each table.

Although this had only taken a few minutes, Rebecca was flushed with heat, and she wiped a few tiny beads of sweat from her forehead. She should not have been flustered by the activity, as it had gone smoothly, so she could only assume that her reaction was to Elijah's close presence.

Now that the tables and benches were set up in the correct places, Rebecca hurried out to the mobile kitchen to help with the food preparation. Her stomach rumbled at the enticing aroma of freshly brewed *kaffi* and roasted chicken. Everywhere she looked, there was food: mountains of mashed potatoes and gravy, hot, creamed celery with real cream, roasted chicken, various salads, cheeses, bread, tapioca pudding, home-canned fruit, pudding, doughnuts, cakes, pies, and copious amounts of ice cream.

"Rebecca!" Mrs. Miller's summons was shrill and demanding.

Rebecca hurried over to her *mudder.*

Mrs. Miller leaned over and whispered to Rebecca in a conspiratorial tone. "Please go and check on the *Ecktenders* for me. You know your *Aenti* Irene is sometimes *ab im kopp*!" Her whisper rose to a high shrill.

Rebecca nodded and hurried out of the mobile kitchen, smiling to herself as she went. Her *Aenti* Irene, a lovely woman, was her *daed's schweschder,* and so was considered far too liberal by Mrs. Miller. Still, she had never heard her *mudder* refer to her as *ab im kopp,* "not right in the head," before; this was no doubt to the pressure of the wedding. *Perhaps Mamm thinks Aenti Irene is going to do something horribly non traditional,* she thought with amusement.

Rebecca walked back in the barn and surveyed the

tables set up around the outskirts of the barn. The bridal party's *Eck* table was still set up correctly in the corner.

Aenti Irene was busy setting Martha's new china set on display. This was the traditional gift from the groom to the bride. Rebecca did not think her *mudder* would quite approve of the china set either. While it was functional, it was no doubt a little too pretty for her *mudder's* liking. Mrs. Miller approved of white china, and perhaps white china with a subtle pattern, but the pattern on this china was far from subtle. The base color was the palest of pinks, and the china was decorated with tiny, little pink rosebuds. Delicate leaves and fronds of gently waving ferns provided the backdrop, but the worst thing of all, Rebecca knew, would be the gold. A slender trimming of gold edged each piece of china, and some of the leaves and fern fronds themselves were actually gold. While the pattern might appear subtle to an *Englischer*, Rebecca knew that it screamed *Unacceptable Break With Tradition* to Mrs. Miller.

Mrs. Miller's closest friend, Mrs. Yoder, scowled as she walked past and directed a disapproving glare at the china. Rebecca wrung her hands with concern. She hoped that the divide between the conservative and the not-so-conservative in the community would not cause any problems at Martha's wedding.

Aenti Irene left the china to arrange the *Eck Schissle* on the table. The *Eck Schissle* were gifts which were given only on the wedding day. Unlike *Englisch* weddings, most Amish wedding gifts were not given on the day of the wedding, but were given in the weeks afterward when the bride and groom spent the traditional post-wedding time visiting other *familyes*, before returning to the Hostetler *haus* where they would live for several months. The gifts would always be practical: farming tools, quilts, and herb and vegetable seeds.

As was traditional, the Hostetler *familye*, being the *familye* of the groom, were to provide the place for the couple to stay for the first few months after marriage, and the Miller *familye*, being the *familye* of the bride, were to provide the necessities for the setting up of their household: the major appliances, furniture, cutlery, crockery, linen, and quilts.

The *Eck Schissle* were filled with brightly colored candy of every description, covered with clear wrap, and tied with colored ribbons. To each one was attached a card with a message from the giver as well as the giver's name.

It was now time for the first shift of the meal. The wedding party, Martha and Moses, Hannah and Noah, and Esther and Jacob, walked into the barn. Martha took up her seat on the left side of Moses. Mr. Miller, the *vadder* of the bride, and Mr. Hostetler, the *vadder* of the groom, sat at the head of the table, and the other male relatives sat on the same side of the table. Opposite them sat Mrs. Miller, the *mudder* of the bride, and Mr. Hostetler, the *mudder* of the groom, and the other female relatives.

Next filed in the young people who were still single. The females walked over to take up their place on Martha's side of the room, and the males went to sit on Moses' side of the room.

The *Ecktenders* at once served the young people.

Weddings were the only occasion where the *youngie*, the young people, were served first. Soon, everyone was served a large meal, and most ate quickly so that the area could be cleared for the next shift. Large platters of mouth-watering roast chicken, roast turkey and baked ham, clouds of creamy mashed potatoes, flavorsome gravy, and creamed celery made with real cream were among the delicious items brought out, soon to be followed by all manner of tasty desserts and copious amounts of homemade ice cream. There were plenty of freshly baked bread rolls, accompanied by freshly churned butter. There was an abundance of *kaffi*, water, and meadow tea. At the end of the meal, Martha and Moses were each served a special tapioca pudding in a wine glass.

The rest of the day went by in a blur for Rebecca: the singing, the games, and the conversation, even the second meal which was served at dusk.

By nightfall Rebecca found herself in the *haus* kitchen washing dishes with *Aenti* Irene. The other women assigned to washing dishes were doing so in the mobile kitchen. Rebecca usually enjoyed time spent with *Aenti* Irene; tonight, however, this was not the case.

"So, Rebecca, how long before you'll be married to Elijah Hostetler?"

Rebecca let out a long breath. "Oh please don't tease me, *Aenti*. I get upset when people keep teasing me about Elijah."

Aenti Irene turned to Rebecca, and held her sudsy hands out of the dishwater for a moment. "I'm not teasing you," she said, her tone perfectly serious. "You're in love with him, aren't you?"

"Why, yes," Rebecca said shyly, looking around to make sure no one could overhear them. "It's just that I don't know if he's in love with me."

Aenti Irene looked puzzled. "What do you mean?"

Rebecca felt at a loss how to explain her innermost thoughts. "Well, I'm worried that Elijah would just fall into marrying me, because everyone expects it, what with my three *schweschders* now married to his three *bruders*."

"But you do want to marry him, don't you?"

Rebecca nodded. "*Jah*, of course I do. But I don't want to marry him if he's only marrying me out of expectation. I want him to be truly in love with me and to marry me just for love."

"Love, pffft!" *Aenti* Irene exclaimed loudly, startling Rebecca. "My advice is to marry him as soon as you can. He can fall in love with you *after* you're married. If you don't marry him at the first opportunity, some other *maidel* will. I've seen the new girl, Sarah, making moon eyes at him. Would you rather Elijah marry her, or you?"

Rebecca stared at her *aenti*. She had not thought it about like that before.

"You take it from me," *Aenti* Irene continued. "I once let a *mann* slip out of my grasp because I didn't know what his reasons for marrying me were. He married someone else, and now I'm all alone. Do you want to be like me, all alone with no *bopplin*?"

Rebecca continued to stare at *Aenti* Irene. She had

always thought that *Aenti* Irene was a happy person, yet she had known nothing of this part of her life. Was *Aenti* Irene right? Should she marry Elijah? Well, he had not asked her to marry him yet, but if he did, should she at once accept without hesitation? Was romantic love a childish concept, after all? Was Rebecca doing the wrong thing in wanting Elijah to love her with all his heart and soul, or would being married to Elijah, if he didn't love her, be enough?

Chapter Eleven

Rebecca arrived at the B&B the day after Martha's wedding with bleary eyes from lack of sleep. Again, she had risen earlier than usual to help with cleaning up after the wedding. Her *mudder* had finally shooed her out of the kitchen to get ready for work.

Mrs. Flickinger was tired too, having helped at the wedding and the wedding preparations the day previously. "Rebecca, would you please prepare the Spinning Star Quilt room for a guest?"

"Sure, how long will he be staying?"

Mrs. Flickinger shrugged her shoulders and rubbed her eyes. "Could be long term. He doesn't know, he said possibly a four-week minimum, but likely much longer."

Rebecca yawned.

"Have a mug of *kaffi* first, dear," Mrs. Flickinger said, nodding to the pot of coffee.

"*Denki*." The aroma of the freshly brewed *kaffi* had made Rebecca wake up somewhat, and drinking a whole mug helped her feel wide awake indeed.

The Spinning Star Quilt room was Rebecca's favorite, and was usually reserved for guests who were staying more than one night. It had a queen-sized bed featuring a beautifully made quilt in jewel colors of bright blue, red and green, along with earthy brown, set against a background of cream. The plain oak headboard only served to show off the quilt in all its beauty. The rest of the room was plain, apart from a working fireplace. There was an old, spindle back rocking chair which had been newly upholstered in fall colors of russet brown, and a practical oak desk in the corner. There was a large, mahogany, two door sectional armoire closet that featured two large beveled mirrors.

Rebecca, who of course had no mirrors in her *haus*, would often stare at herself in the mirrors in the armoire. At first she had felt guilty, but had soon told herself that she was not looking for reasons of vanity, but rather, simply out of curiosity. Today she took in the appearance of her puffy eyes, and the dark circles under them. "I need more sleep," she said aloud to herself, and then immediately looked over her shoulder. To her relief, there was no sign of Nash Grayson, so she set herself to vacuuming the carpet.

When the room was vacuumed and thoroughly dusted and otherwise thoroughly prepared, Rebecca went in search of Mrs. Flickinger for further instruction. She found her at the desk, checking in a tall Amish *mann*.

Mrs. Flickinger looked up at her approach. "Oh, *gut*, Rebecca. Would you please show our guest to his room?

This is Benjamin Shetler. Benjamin, I'd like you to meet Rebecca, Rebecca Miller."

Rebecca quickly assessed Benjamin's appearance. He looked kind and nice, and was tall, with sandy colored hair, big brown eyes, and broad shoulders. Rebecca figured him to be a farmer, used to hard physical work. "*Jah*, certainly. Which room is that?"

Mrs. Flickinger raised her eyebrows as if Rebecca had gone *ferhoodled*. "The Spinning Star Quilt room, as we discussed."

Rebecca nodded, feeling quite foolish. She knew, of course, that a guest was expected that morning, but she had no idea that the guest Mrs. Flickinger had mentioned would be a young Amish *mann*. For some reason, she had expected the guest to be *Englisch*.

Benjamin appeared to be friendly and chatty. "Is it always this cold here for this time of year?" he asked on the way to his room.

Rebecca shook her head. "*Nee*. It looks like an early winter, for sure."

"Was it your *schweschder* who was married yesterday?"

"*Jah*."

Rebecca wondered why Mrs. Flickinger had told him that there had been a wedding the day before. *Perhaps it was to explain why she was so tired*, she thought. As Benjamin was so forthcoming, Rebecca thought it fine to ask him a question. "So where are you from?"

They had reached the door to his room, and both stood there for a moment, not speaking. Rebecca wondered if he would answer her question.

Finally he said, "Out of town," before averting his eyes.

Well, obviously, Rebecca thought, feeling a little bad that she had pressed him for information. Nevertheless that did not stop her asking one final question. "So, are you on *rumspringa*?"

"Sort of, something like that," Benjamin said, before smiling at her, and walking through the doorway. "*Denki* for showing me to my room," he said as he shut the door.

Rebecca stood in the hallway, puzzled. Why was Benjamin Shetler being so secretive? Perhaps his community was not so *schnell*, as her *mudder* called the not-so-conservative. *How can someone be 'sort of' on rumspringa?* Rebecca silently asked herself. *You are either on rumspringa or not on rumspringa. You can't be on 'something like' rumspringa.*

Ida Flickinger was in the kitchen, sitting at the table and drinking *kaffi*. Her shoulders were slumped and she looked awfully tired.

"Would you like me to do the laundry now?"

"*Jah, denki*."

Rebecca made to leave the kitchen, but then turned back. "The new guest is 'sort of' on *rumspringa*."

Rebecca expected Ida to ask her what she meant, but Ida merely said, "He arrived here with the bishop in the bishop's buggy."

"He did?"

Ida simply nodded and sipped more *kaffi*. Rebecca did not like to discuss the matter with her. After all, Mrs. Flickinger had enough problems with her son, Nash Grayson, and looked like she needed a *gut* sleep.

Rebecca walked to the laundry room, her thoughts full of Benjamin Shetler. What a mystery he was turning out to be!

After the laundry was done, Rebecca took a pot of peppermint tea and a dish of pot pie up to *Grossmammi* Deborah's room. Today *Grossmammi* was doing better than usual, and was sitting up in bed, propped up by several pillows. "Rebecca," she said in a weak voice, "please sit down and tell me all about the wedding."

Rebecca enjoyed her chats with *grossmammi*, although they were always brief as *grossmammi* became tired so easily. After Rebecca gave *grossmammi* a brief run down of the wedding, she told her what *Aenti* Irene had said about Elijah.

Grossmammi's eyes sparkled. "See, child, that's what I've been telling you all along."

Rebecca sighed. *Grossmammi* Deborah had indeed been telling Rebecca that she should marry Elijah, even if he wasn't in love with her.

"Love will come later," *Grossmammi* said again.

"But what if it doesn't, *Grossmammi*?" Rebecca asked, looking down at her apron and twisting it between her hands. "What if Elijah never does fall in love with me, and I have to live in a loveless marriage forever?" When no answer was forthcoming, Rebecca looked at *Grossmammi* only to see that she had fallen asleep.

Rebecca walked downstairs to polish the silver. Soon Mrs. Flickinger joined her at the old oak table in the kitchen. They were still there polishing silverware an hour later, when Nash walked into the room. Rebecca gave a little jump.

Nash narrowed his eyes and did not speak for a few moments. Rebecca waited for him to say something. Finally, he said, "You're polishing silverware."

"Yes," his mother said in a small voice.

"I thought you wanted people to come here to have the Amish experience? Isn't that why you don't have Wi-Fi?"

"We do have Wi-Fi," Rebecca said with a sigh.

"You do?" Nash pulled his phone out of the pocket and tapped away at the screen. "Oh yes, I see there's an available network. Can I have the password?"

Rebecca noticed that he hadn't said 'please', but Mrs. Flickinger said, "I will fetch it for you."

Rebecca jumped to her feet. "*Nee*, I'll fetch it."

It didn't take her long to retrieve the password. She wondered why Mrs. Flickinger hadn't left the card with the Wi-Fi password in Nash's room.

She handed it to Nash, and he did thank her when he took it. "So you don't really want people to have the Amish experience, do you? You have electricity, Wi-Fi, and you even have silverware."

Mrs. Flickinger put her head down and polished the silverware even more furiously, so Rebecca felt she should explain. "Guests still have an Amish experience. They're in Amish country on an old Amish farm, and your parents, the hosts, are Amish. The guests have a full Amish breakfast and they have Amish quilts in their room. Besides, you very well know that Amish businesses are permitted to have electricity."

Nash rolled his eyes and tossed his head. "Whatever! Anyway, I'm bored so I decided I would help with the B&B."

Mrs. Flickinger's mouth fell open. "Help?" she repeated, and then she smiled.

Rebecca was not so trusting and wondered why Nash's own mother was. Rebecca was sure Nash was up to something.

"Yes, I'm bored," he said again. "I want do something to help. Could I paint a room?"

"Do you know how to paint?" his mother asked, seemingly concerned.

Nash nodded. "Sure, it's one of the odd jobs I had for a while."

"The west sitting room does need painting," Mrs. Flickinger said. "Let's go and look at it now. Come along, Rebecca."

Rebecca walked after Mrs. Flickinger and Nash into the west sitting room. It was quite bare and was one of the rooms the Flickingers hadn't quite got around to redecorating. It had lovely French doors out onto the garden, but the room itself was drab. Rebecca swept it on a regular basis so it was clean.

"This will do nicely," Nash said with what Rebecca judged to be genuine enthusiasm in his voice.

Maybe I have misjudged him, she thought. *Maybe he's like the prodigal son from the Bible and he will turn out to be good, after all.* As soon as she thought the words, she was immediately filled with reservations.

"I can I paint all the walls then?" Nash said.

"Sure," his mother said.

"And what about the furniture?"

"It already has some furniture," Mrs. Flickinger said, nodding to a sideboard.

Nash walked over to look at the sideboard. "So, is this sideboard staying in this room?" he asked his mother.

"*Jah*," she said. "And so is the chest of drawers and the blanket chest."

Nash nodded slowly. "I can work with this," he said, "and the room needs more furniture. What about a TV?"

"A TV?" Mrs. Flickinger began and she would have said more, but Nash interrupted her.

"If you're going to have Wi-Fi then you really need TV."

"There are so many things for the guest to do," Mrs. Flickinger said. "There are plenty of outdoor activities and at night they can read."

Nash waved one finger at her. "Trust me. They won't be reading at night unless it's on their phones or their tablets. They will be watching TV on their tablets, so you might not need TVs in the rooms, but you need a big one in the sitting room."

Mrs. Flickinger looked doubtful. "I don't know. I'll have to ask your *vadder*."

It seemed to Rebecca that Nash was growing annoyed and doing his best to hide it.

"Well, let's get this organised. Where will I get the paint?"

"All the gardening supplies are in the barn and there are several gallons of paint there as well."

Nash's face fell. Rebecca wondered if he wanted his

mother to give him money for paint and then he would go and do something unsavoury with it. Whatever it was, it seemed the fact that Mrs. Flickinger already had paint had spoiled his Nash's plans in some way.

"All right, I'll make a start," he said. "Can I buy some extra stuff for the room?"

"We don't have any money for the room." Mrs. Flickinger wrung her hands. "I hadn't been planning on redecorating it yet."

Nash leaned against the sideboard and patted it. "What if I sell something you don't really need, in order to pay for stuff for the room?"

Mrs. Flickinger bit her lip. "I suppose so," she said in a worried tone.

Nash smiled and hurried through the French doors. Mrs. Flickinger and Rebecca walked back to the kitchen to resume polishing silverware. "I'm pleased Eli wanted to help," Mrs. Flickinger said to Rebecca.

Rebecca nodded. "*Jah*," was all she said. She was certain Nash didn't want to help at all. She was certain he had his own agenda. But what could it be?

She was still polishing silverware, when Benjamin Shetler came into the room. Both women looked up at him, but Mrs. Flickinger was the first to speak. "I hope everything is to your liking, Mr. Shetler."

"*Jah, denki*," he said. "Please call me Benjamin."

"Would you like some meadow tea and Fasnachts?" Mrs. Flickinger asked him. "Rebecca and I were just about to take a break."

"That would be *wunderbar, denki*," Benjamin said. "I haven't had Fasnachts for ages."

"Rebecca makes them for the guests."

Rebecca had made some triangular-shaped Fasnachts only that morning. She had deep fried the potato and then coated it with granular sugar, before filling them with raspberry jelly.

Soon, the three of them were sitting on the porch, sipping meadow tea and eating Fasnachts.

Mr. Flickinger walked around the side of the building. Mrs. Flickinger called out to him and then hurried over to him. Rebecca figured she was asking him about Nash's request for a TV.

"So, your three sisters are married now," Benjamin said to Rebecca.

"*Jah*, they are," she said with a chuckle. "I'm the last one left. I'm all alone."

"But you're not alone. You have Sarah and Mary," he pointed out.

Rebecca laughed. "Yes, that's true. I meant I was the last one of my *schweschders*."

"So, what's it like having Sarah and Mary living with you?"

"It's good," Rebecca said. "They're both good company. I'd be sad if they weren't living at home now that Hannah, Esther, and Martha are all married. Mary lives in the *grossmammi haus*, but Sarah lives in our house, and the three of us spend a lot of time together."

Benjamin nodded slowly. "And do Sarah and Mary seem happy away from their homes?"

"Sure," Rebecca said, wondering why he was asking such questions.

"I enjoyed dinner at your house the other night,"

Benjamin continued. "Your mother seems very fond of Sarah. Oh, and Mary."

"*Jah*, she is." Rebecca wished that if Benjamin wanted to know something that he would come straight out and ask her, rather than trying to make small talk. She was certain he had something on his mind. She was on the point of asking him what it was, when she saw Nash hurrying down the road, leading the Flickinger's buggy horse.

"I wonder what he's doing with that horse?" Benjamin said.

"How strange," Rebecca said. "He's walking awfully fast too. Where would he be taking the horse?"

She wondered if she should go and tell the Flickingers, but she figured they must already know.

"Maybe he's taking the horse for some grass," Benjamin said.

"There's plenty of grass in the horse's field." Rebecca slipped one hand under her bonnet and scratched her head. "Maybe he just wants to spend time with the horse. He does love animals. It's his one redeeming feature." With that, she covered her mouth with her hand. "I didn't mean to say that."

Benjamin laughed heartily. "That's fine. I haven't really met anyone like Nash before. *Er hot net der glaawe.*" *He doesn't keep up the faith.*

"I haven't met anyone like him either," Rebecca admitted. She felt quite tense speaking with Benjamin and hoped Mrs. Flickinger would soon return.

"Does Sarah ever talk about her former community?" Benjamin suddenly asked her.

Rebecca wondered why he was so interested in Sarah. Maybe he had taken an instant liking to her and that was why he wanted to know more about her. Rebecca nodded to herself. Yes, that must be it. "I don't actually think she's ever said anything about her old community," Rebecca said. "I know Martha met her when they were both on *rumspringa*."

Just then, Mrs. Flickinger returned. She picked up her meadow tea and walked into the house. Rebecca followed her. She was glad to escape from Benjamin and all his questioning.

Hours later, after Rebecca finished doing the laundry, she thought she would check on the west sitting room to see if Nash was indeed making any progress. The door was locked. She knocked on it several times before she got a response. "Who's there?" Nash's voice said.

"Rebecca," she said.

Nash opened the door a little. "It's a surprise. I don't want anyone to see it."

"All right." Rebecca's spirits sank. She did want to see what was going on that room. On the other hand, she was pleased Nash was actually working for once.

Chapter Twelve

When Rebecca arrived back at the Miller *haus* after work that day, the cleaning up after the wedding had all been done. The only person in sight was Sarah, who was sitting at the big oak table in the kitchen, sipping a mug of hot meadow tea. Rebecca knew her *daed* would still be at work in the barn, but wondered where her *mudder*, Martha, and Moses were.

She walked over to Sarah and stretched widely, before yawning. "Where is everyone?"

Sarah looked up and smiled. "Your *mudder* and Mary are over at the Yoders' *haus*, and Martha and Moses are out visiting."

"Already? They didn't waste any time."

Sarah simply nodded, so Rebecca went to make herself a nice hot cup of meadow tea. Having done so, she returned to the table and sat down.

"So, tell me all about Nash Grayson," Sarah asked.

Rebecca was surprised. "But you've already met him. What do you want to know?"

Sarah shrugged. “Everyone’s sorry for poor Mrs. Flickinger, what with her *sohn* gone all wild, and her *mudder* so ill. Everyone was talking about it yesterday, at the wedding. So, what’s he like when he’s at the B&B?”

Rebecca chewed her lip. “Well, I haven’t seen much of him, really, but he seems…” Rebecca searched for the words and then continued, “Nice enough, I suppose. He’s polite, at any rate.”

“Perhaps he’ll fall in love with you and return to the community.”

Rebecca pulled a face. “Not funny, Sarah, not funny. Why is everyone so keen to get me married off? You just wait until *Mamm* starts trying to find a *mann* for you, and then you won’t be laughing.”

Sarah thought that remark was highly amusing. “Well, you must admit he’s *gut* looking.”

Rebecca giggled. “*Jah*, he sure is, and talking of *gut* looking *menner*, the B&B seems to attract them, because the guest who came today is just as handsome as Nash, maybe even more so.”

“Maybe you’ll abandon Elijah for him.”

Rebecca stopped chuckling and gave Sarah a long, hard look. Was Sarah interested in Elijah for herself? Was this Sarah’s way of asking Rebecca whether or not she was interested in Elijah? Rebecca had no idea how to respond, so changed the subject. “There’s a bit of mystery with this *mann* though, Sarah,” she said in lowered tones. “The bishop drove him to the B&B in his buggy.”

Sarah's whole face changed at once. "What, he's Amish?" she asked in a horrified voice.

Rebecca wondered why Sarah appeared upset about the B&B having an Amish guest. "*Jah*. He's tall and handsome, with big brown eyes like Hannah's beagle, and he has fair hair. Clean shaven too, so he's single. Maybe you should check him out." Rebecca added the last sentence to see if Sarah would give any indication as to whether she was interested in a new, handsome *mann*. If she did, that would mean that she wasn't interested in Elijah, after all, and Rebecca would be able to breathe a sigh of relief. Rebecca closely watched Sarah for her reaction. However, Sarah was suddenly serious, and stood up. The mood in the kitchen had suddenly changed to one of tension.

Sarah leaned over the table. "What's his name?"

"Benjamin Shetler." Rebecca looked down at her tea, a little disappointed that her ploy hadn't worked. She was none the wiser as to how Sarah felt about Elijah. When Rebecca looked up, Sarah was clutching at her stomach and swaying. "Sarah!" she exclaimed. "Are you all right? You've gone as white as a sheet! You look like you're going to faint."

When Sarah didn't answer, Rebecca took her by the arm and helped her into the living room. "Here, lie down! I'll get you a glass of water."

When Rebecca returned with the water, a little color had returned to Sarah's face.

"*Denki*, Rebecca. I don't know what's wrong with me. Perhaps I forgot to eat today. What were we talking about?"

"Benjamin Shetler." This time, Rebecca's mention of the name had no effect on Sarah. Rebecca had at first thought that Sarah must know the *mann*. Now she thought that Sarah's fainting turn when she had said his name was just a coincidence.

"Did you say Benjamin Shetler?"

Both girls looked up as Mrs. Miller hurried into the kitchen.

"Yes, *Mamm*."

"Well, what do you know about him, Rebecca?" Mrs. Miller demanded. "Did Ida Flickinger tell you anything about him?"

"*Nee*, she didn't appear to know anything much herself."

Mrs. Miller poured herself a hot meadow tea and sat down with the girls. "I've just come from Betsy Yoder's. She told me that Benjamin Shetler had been to see the bishop, and the bishop himself drove him to the B&B. Why would a young Amish *mann* from another community go to see our bishop?"

Rebecca thought for a moment. "Perhaps he was shunned, and wants to come back to the Amish, but is too embarrassed to go back to his community, so wants to make a fresh start somewhere else."

Mrs. Miller nodded her approval. "Could be, that could be one possible reason. Anyway, I don't like it, I don't like it all, outsiders forcing their way into our community."

"*Mamm!*" Rebecca was shocked, as Sarah and Mary were sitting right there.

Mrs. Miller's expression turned black. "Don't be so

silly, Rebecca, you should know better. Obviously I don't mean Sarah or Mary! They're part of the *familye* now. You should think before you speak. Now you've embarrassed Sarah, and Mary too."

Rebecca held her tongue. There was no use trying to reason with her *mudder* at times like this.

Mary was distracted, looking at Sarah's cat. Sarah murmured that she was not embarrassed, but Mrs. Miller cut her off. "We will invite this Benjamin Shetler to dinner, and see what he has to say for himself."

Rebecca could not help but notice that Sarah's face had turned deathly white again.

Chapter Thirteen

Nash did the math as he led the Flickinger's horse, Henry, down the road. He had been able to source the items he needed at a reasonable price. They were used items, but he had already inspected them and they did look as good as new. No one would guess they were used.

After walking for an hour, he was beginning to have second thoughts. "How much further can this widow live?" he complained to the horse. "It didn't look so far on the map app on my phone." He pulled his phone out of his jeans pocket to consult it. Just then a car sped by, startling Nash rather than the horse. Nash shook his fist and let out a string of language at the car. It made him feel good because he had to watch what he said around his parents, and he wasn't used to censoring his language.

When he finally found the lane leading to the Widow Ramseyer's house, he let out a loud yell of relief. He was soon was stricken by a horrible thought that maybe the widow wasn't home.

"She can't go anywhere, because she doesn't have a horse," he said aloud. "Then again, maybe some of these do-gooders took her out for coffee or something." He shrugged. He had come this far—he might as well push on.

Nash had worn a long shirt so as to cover his tattoos, and he had removed his nose ring and piercings. As he approached the widow Ramseyer's house, he squinted to see if he could see her anywhere. Alas, he couldn't. He looked for her in the vegetable garden, but she wasn't there, so he tied the horse to the hitching post and walked up the steps. Just as his hand was raised to knock, a woman opened the door. She gasped when she saw him.

"I am Samuel and Ida Flickinger's son," Nash announced. When she looked blank, he added, "I'm on *rumspringa*."

The woman at once looked relieved. She smiled warmly. "I'm Rhoda Ramseyer. Of course, you know that, or you wouldn't have come here."

"Have you met my parents?"

She nodded slowly. "Yes, at the meetings."

Nash nodded. "Anyway, I've come here today because my parents and I were having dinner at the Millers' house the other night—you know, Abraham and Rachel Miller. Mr. Miller told us that your mare has gone lame."

Mrs. Ramseyer's face at once crumpled. "Yes, poor

Susan. She'll be no use to anyone now, but she can live out her days in the fields."

"Well, I'll come straight to the point. Would you like to buy a good buggy horse?" He pointed to Henry. "He is nice and quiet."

Mrs. Ramseyer walked out the door and looked at the horse. "He looks a good horse, but I'm afraid I don't have much money."

"My parents were upset that you didn't have a buggy horse, so they said you could have him for one thousand dollars." Nash knew he was exaggerating horrendously, but he didn't care.

The woman's hand flew to her throat. "But a good buggy horse like that is worth so much more!"

"My parents couldn't afford to give him to you, but they were hoping you can afford one thousand dollars. They need the money for their bed and breakfast business."

"Yes I do have a thousand dollars to buy a horse, but I knew I wouldn't be able to get one for that price," she said, "only an unbroken one, and I'm certainly not going to buy a horse like that."

"Why don't you let me harness him and we can take him for a drive?"

Mrs. Ramseyer clasped her hands. "That would be *wunderbar*!"

It didn't take long for Nash to harness the horse to Mrs. Ramseyer's buggy. After all, he had been raised Amish and it was only in the last few years that he had gone on *rumspringa*. Of course, he was not going to stay on *rumspringa* forever. He laughed at his little private joke.

He helped Mrs. Ramseyer into the buggy. She was quite frail. He thought it was hard for her, with no one around to help her. It even crossed his mind to give her the horse for free, but then again, he had said he was going to redecorate the room and he needed money to do that.

"I'll show you how reliable he is with traffic," Nash said. He let the horse plod along at a nice clip. "What do you think of him?"

"He seems ideal," Mrs. Ramseyer said. "I can't believe *Gott* has sent me a horse that I can afford."

"Now let's go out on the road, and I'll show you how good he is," Nash said. It wasn't long before a truck went past a little too fast. Henry didn't react at all.

"He *is* very reliable," Mrs. Ramseyer said. "He's just as reliable as Susan."

"He's sound too," Nash said. "He's got a lot more years in him and he's very friendly. He likes lots of pats and grooming." Nash did not add that he had spent some time with the horse, and he would miss him. Nash preferred horses to people.

"Would you like to drive him now?" he asked Mrs. Ramseyer.

"Yes, I think that would be good."

Soon Mrs. Ramseyer was driving the buggy back to her house, commenting on how good the horse was. "So then, do you want to buy him?" Nash asked.

"Yes I do," she said. "Can you leave him with me now?"

"Sure," Nash said, wondering when she was going to hand over the cash.

"I can give you the cash right now," she said.

Nash tried not to smile too widely.

"And then I'll drive you home. Are you living at the B&B?"

"No!" Nash said hurriedly, and then amended that to, "I mean yes, but there's no need to drive me home, but thanks for your kind offer. I enjoy walking in the fresh air. It gives me a chance to think."

Mrs. Ramseyer nodded slowly. "Yes, a good chance to think and pray."

"Err, yes," Nash said.

"I insist you have lunch with me before you go," Mrs. Ramseyer said as she brought the horse to a stop the front of the house.

"That would be excellent," Nash said. "I'll unharness Henry. Where would you like me to put him?"

"In that field there," she said. She got out and stroked the horse's neck. Nash was pleased to see that Henry seemed to like her. He was happy Henry had gone to a good home. He would miss him though, but he did need the cash and Mrs. Ramseyer did need the horse. It was perfect.

After Nash unharnessed the horse, Mrs. Ramseyer showed him to a large wooden table in the kitchen. "Sit down, dear. Have some lemonade and some Shoo-fly pie while I make some lunch."

Nash was starving. He'd had to fend for himself since he'd left the Amish, and things had been tough. He ate half the Shoo-fly pie and wondered if he could keep going. No, he thought, he should save some room for lunch.

Mrs. Ramseyer returned and set before him a large bowl of chicken pot pie.

"Eat up," she urged him. "You young people never eat enough, and you're too thin. You need meat on your bones. Eat!"

Nash didn't need to be told twice. As soon as he polished off his meal, Mrs. Ramseyer heaped more into his bowl.

Nash ate until he could hardly eat any more, and Mrs. Ramseyer looked quite pleased with herself. Would you like some apple dumplings?" she asked him.

Nash's belt was tight, and he didn't know if he could eat anything else but apple dumplings did sound awfully good.

"*Denki*," he said.

"One serving won't hurt you," Mrs. Ramseyer said, "and have some lemonade with it to help it go down."

After he had finished, she urged him to eat some more. "That was a lovely meal, but I don't think I can fit one more thing in," Nash said honestly.

"Why, it is a long walk back to your parents' *haus*. I'll give you something to eat along the way." Mrs. Ramseyer disappeared to the kitchen and then came back. "Here you are." She handed him a large bag. "I've given you Shoo-fly pies, whoopie pies, and sugar cakes. That walk will make you hungry."

"Thanks," Nash said. Mrs. Ramseyer was the nicest person he had met since he had come to this community.

"And come here any time for a chat," she said. "I get

awfully lonely and bored. I'll give you a big feed. I'm sure you'll miss your horse, so come back and see him."

"Thanks. You know, I think I'll take you up on your offer."

Mrs. Ramseyer's face lit up.

Nash said goodbye to Mrs. Ramseyer and set off at slow walk in the direction of the B&B. "What a nice woman," he said aloud. "I wish everyone was like her. I'll go back and visit her for sure." Nash once more wished he could have given her the horse for free, but now he had the cash, and he would have to go and buy that TV and the couch before they were sold to someone else. Also, he had to buy paint. There was no way he was going to use the dreadfully pale, insipid paint that his parents wanted him to use to paint the walls. No, he needed the room to be memorable.

And it sure is going to be memorable, he thought, and then laughed aloud.

Chapter Fourteen

Rebecca was sweeping the front porch of the B&B when Nash Grayson appeared and sat down in one of the chairs. "What a lovely view," he said. His voice dripped charm.

Rebecca was relieved that she had already swept under the chairs, as she didn't fancy having to ask him to move. "Yes it is, but you should see it just before harvest, when the fields of corn look beautiful."

"I wasn't talking about the landscape."

Rebecca was puzzled at first and then embarrassed. *Is he flirting with me?* she wondered.

Nash was clearly amused by her embarrassment. "Will you have dinner with me?"

"*Nee*," Rebecca said automatically, and then wondered if that was rude. "My *mudder* has guests for dinner tonight."

Nash waved a hand absently. "I don't mean tonight, I mean at some point in the future."

"*Nee*," Rebecca said again, "but *denki* for asking."

She looked at Nash to see how he would react, and saw what she thought was a calculating look pass across his face.

"Is it Elijah Hostetler?" he asked.

Rebecca put her head down and swept briskly, not wishing to pursue this conversation, but Nash got out of his chair and walked over to her. Rebecca's stomach clenched, wondering what he was about to say, but Mr. Flickinger thankfully chose this moment to tell Rebecca that Mrs. Flickinger needed her help with *Grossmammi* Deborah.

Nash watched Rebecca hurry away. He also saw yet another stern look of disapproval pass across his father's face before he followed Rebecca into the building. Whatever. His behavior was no doubt as he was stressed, and that stress was his parents' fault for not helping him out with his debts.

Nash returned to his seat and sat back down, looking across at the open fields. He wished he could return to city life and get away from the dreary, boring countryside, but right now he didn't have enough money to do so. He would have to look for work, and then save up enough money to return to the city. Lucky for him he was getting free board at his parents' B&B, but he was bored out of his mind. Didn't these people do anything for fun?

His thoughts turned to Rebecca. Why had she refused his invitation for dinner? She was the first girl who had ever refused him. Clearly it was because she was Amish. Had she not been Amish, she would no doubt have accepted his invitation in a flash. Nash thought some more. Or was the reason in fact that she was in love with Elijah? He had seen the looks Elijah shot his way when he had spoken to Rebecca the day before the wedding.

Nash smiled to himself. He had the spark of an idea how to liven things up around here. This community would soon change from the boring place it was now.

Benjamin Shetler looked decidedly uncomfortable, Rebecca thought, despite her *mudder's* uncharacteristic warm tone in addressing him. He was already at the Miller *haus* when Rebecca arrived home from work, and as Moses and Martha were away visiting, as was the Amish custom for newlyweds, and as Sarah and Mary were nowhere to be seen, Benjamin and Mrs. Miller were engaging in what looked like awkward conversation.

"*Hullo, Mamm. Hullo*, Benjamin."

Benjamin stood and greeted Rebecca.

"Where are Sarah and Mary?" Rebecca asked.

Mrs. Miller looked behind Rebecca. "I'm expecting them any minute now. They walked over to help Hannah with the twins."

As if on cue, Sarah walked through the door, looking hot and flustered, despite the cool air. She walked straight over to Benjamin. "*Hullo*, nice to meet you. I'm Sarah Beachy."

Benjamin looked taken aback, or so Rebecca thought. "Err, *hiya,* Sarah," he stammered. "I'm Benjamin Shetler."

Sarah gave Benjamin a curt nod and then turned to

Mrs. Miller. "Sorry I'm late. What can I do to help prepare the meal?"

Mrs. Miller stood up. "*Nee, nee.* You two girls stay here and talk to Benjamin. Mary and I will see to the dinner." With that, Mrs. Miller hurried out of the room, leaving Rebecca to wonder with whom her *mudder* wanted to pair Benjamin: her, or Sarah. Her *mudder* was not happy unless she was matchmaking.

No one spoke for a while, which made Rebecca somewhat nervous. She cleared her throat. "So, how are you liking our community, Benjamin?"

"*Gut, denki.*"

Rebecca's face fell as her attempt to make conversation had fallen so flat. She tried again. "Have you met Nash Grayson yet?"

"*Jah.*"

Rebecca pushed on. "Mrs. Flickinger is lovely, isn't she?"

"*Jah.*"

To Rebecca's relief, her *mudder* returned to the table and sat down. "Dinner is ready, we just have to wait for my husband. Benjamin, will you be staying at the B&B long?"

Benjamin squirmed in his seat. "I'm not sure just yet, Mrs. Miller."

"Do you have business concerns here?"

Benjamin continued to squirm. "*Nee.*"

Mrs. Miller appeared not at all put off by Benjamin's obvious attempts to avoid her questions. "Benjamin, why have you come to our community?"

Benjamin's face flushed a deep shade of beet red,

and he looked at the floor. "Forgive me, Mrs. Miller, but what I'm doing here involves someone else, so I am not at liberty to talk about it."

Mrs. Miller rushed to reassure him. "Of course not, Benjamin, please forgive me for asking."

Rebecca hid a smile behind her hand. She knew her *mudder* was determined to find out more about Benjamin, and would indeed find out one way or another.

The unsuspecting Benjamin now looked quite relaxed, and he and Mrs. Miller chatted away happily. He told her that he had come from dairy farming country, but that he wanted to open his own B&B at some point in the future.

"You'll need a *fraa* for that," Mrs. Miller said, causing Rebecca to groan inwardly.

Rebecca glanced at Sarah, expecting her to look amused, but Sarah's face was white and drawn, and she was chewing her fingernails.

Everyone turned to the sound of the front door opening. It was Mr. Miller who appeared to have finished work a little early.

"Rebecca, go and ask Mary to fix your *daed* a hot meadow tea."

"*Jah, Mamm.*" Rebecca was pleased to be out of the room. At least she had a small time in which she would not be embarrassed by her *mudder's* obvious attempts to match her with the new boy in town. Her *mudder* knew nothing about him, but that did not stop her clumsy attempts at matching her with Benjamin.

From the kitchen she could hear her *daed* trying to talk to the young man, but her *mudder* kept cutting across the conversation. Rebecca sighed. *Nothing ever changes around here*, she thought. It appeared that her *mudder* was the only person in the community who did not assume that she would marry Elijah. Mrs. Miller had been most put out when her *dochders* married the Hostetler boys, one by one, although her attitude had changed for the better when Hannah had the twins.

Surely her *mudder* would be pleased for her if she did marry Elijah? Rebecca carried her *daed's* favorite meadow tea carefully to where he sat, and she was just in time to hear him ask Benjamin, "So what is it that brings you here, Benjamin?"

Her *mudder* moved her head forward, as if doing so would help draw the information out of him.

Benjamin's eyes darted about the room. It was clear that he was nervous and trying to hide something. "I'm running an errand for someone."

"I see, someone from your community I suppose?" Mr. Miller asked.

Benjamin nodded, and quickly changed the subject. "I hear you have a successful furniture business, Mr. Miller."

Mr. Miller nodded his head to Rebecca who had just passed him his tea, then chuckled in a low tone at Benjamin's comment. "It keeps the *familye*. *Gott* has blessed us."

"What kind of furniture do you make?" Benjamin shifted position in his seat.

Rebecca had the feeling that he was not the slightest bit interested in her *daed's* business; it was simply a diversion so he would not have to speak about his reasons for visiting the community.

Rebecca's mind wandered while her *daed* talked of all the furniture he made. She was sure he could talk two hours straight about his furniture and the quality of the craftsmanship. Her *mudder's* eyes were glazed over as they usually were when anyone else was speaking, but Rebecca could not help but notice that Sarah was still looking pale and appeared to be nervous. Maybe Sarah was attracted to Benjamin?

"So you're interested in furniture, are you?" Mr. Miller asked.

Benjamin nodded enthusiastically.

"Come out to the barn and I'll show you the workshop."

"No you don't, Abraham. Benjamin is our dinner guest and has come for conversation and *gut* food. You can show him the workshop some other time." Mrs. Miller turned to Benjamin and smiled sweetly. "I take it you will be coming back to visit us since you'll be staying in the community for a while, won't you?"

"*Jah, jah,* of course, *denki*. I'd love to come again."

Rebecca thought his response far too eager. There was something not right about Benjamin and his reasons for being in Lancaster County. She could not figure out what it was. Her *mudder* was not the only one who was intrigued by his presence.

Chapter Fifteen

"Have you seen Eli?" Mrs. Flickinger asked Rebecca.

It took Rebecca a moment to realize Eli was Nash. It could sure get confusing. "*Nee*," she said. "Maybe he is still redecorating the room."

"He wouldn't let me see it," Mrs. Flickinger said.

Just then Eli walked in the room. "Well, it's all ready for you to see now."

Mrs. Flickinger stood up, her face filled with concern. Rebecca too wondered what on earth the sitting room would look like.

They had only taken a step when Nash held up one hand, palm outward, to forestall them. "Now, you both might not like this room at first, but you have to remember that you're running a business. It's not personal taste that counts."

Mrs. Flickinger's face turned pale. "What do you mean?" she asked him.

"I mean it might not be to your taste." He chuckled

and then added, "I mean it *won't* be to your taste, not at all, but the guests will like it. I have modernized it."

Rebecca gasped. She didn't know what Eli meant by *modernized*, but she was sure it couldn't be good.

"Follow me," he said happily.

Rebecca and Mrs. Flickinger hurried to the west sitting room. In fact, Mrs. Flickinger got there before Nash. Mrs. Flickinger was a few paces ahead of Rebecca when Rebecca heard an ear-piercing shriek. She pushed past Nash into the room.

Rebecca was aware her mouth had fallen open in shock. The ceiling was black and the walls were a purple color, the color of newly squashed grapes, only much darker. The three original items of furniture—at least Rebecca guessed that's what they were—were painted in the most hideous shade of vibrant, fluorescent green Rebecca had ever seen.

Nash must have followed her gaze, because he said proudly, "They glow in the dark."

Rebecca spotted one piece of furniture in the room that was presentable. It was a big, brown leather couch. It looked good, Rebecca thought, but it had cushions on it. Printed on the cushions were strange sayings such as, 'Too pretty to pay,' and, 'Born free, but now I'm expensive.'

Over the fluorescent green chest of drawers was a huge sign that said, 'I used to miss my husband, but then my aim improved.'

A huge, flat-screen television dominated one wall and a jukebox stood resplendent in a corner. Rebecca knew what it was, because there was one at the café not far from the apartment market Martha had shared with Cheryl Garner when she was on *rumspringa*.

"Well, do you like it?" Nash said. "There's a lot of damage to the back of the TV, but you can't see it from the front and it works fine. That's how I got it so cheap."

Rebecca didn't know whether Nash was genuinely trying to help, or whether he was being mean. She suspected he was being mean, but maybe he just had appalling taste.

"It's, um, it's..." were the only words Mrs. Flickinger was able to get out. She sat, or rather fell backward, onto the couch. She pulled a cushion out from behind her, read the words on it, and then quickly turned it upside down next to her.

"Do you think it's too much?" Nash asked.

Rebecca did not want to get between the mother and her son but thought perhaps she should say something as Mrs. Flickinger had clearly lost her voice from the shock.

"It's very creative," Rebecca said slowly, as if speaking to a young child, "but your mother is probably shocked, as she would not have seen anything like this before."

"It was hard to get all this stuff delivered today," Nash said, waving his hands around. "I've put a lot of work into it."

"I can see that," Rebecca said. Perhaps he was genuine about helping. "Yes, the painting job is quite good. I can see you're a good painter." She could not resist adding, "But why a black ceiling and purple walls?"

"Because I watch a lot of those home renovation

shows on TV," Nash said. "They always say you should decorate a room so that people will remember it. People will remember this room."

"That's for sure!" Mrs. Flickinger had finally found her voice. She then clutched the cushion to her and buried her face in it.

Rebecca walked around the room, looking at all the items. She thought it all rather strange. Surely it could have been modernized without going to these extremes, but who would want to modernize a lovely old Mennonite building anyway? She had serious reservations about Nash's motivations.

Mrs. Flickinger finally stood up. "Thank you for doing all this hard work, Eli," she said.

Rebecca's heart went out to her. Clearly, she was trying to encourage her son and was giving him the benefit of the doubt.

He crossed his arms over his chest. "You don't like it, do you? You're just being polite. In fact, I think you hate it." His tone held accusation.

"It's just not what I'm used to," Mrs. Flickinger said. "How did you pay for all this?" She nodded to the huge-flat screen television.

Nash pouted. "You said I could sell something you didn't really need. And that's what I did."

Rebecca wondered what Nash could have possibly sold to get the money. She remembered when he had asked his mother if he could sell something to fund the redecorating, and he had been leaning on the chest of drawers at the time. Yet here the chest of drawers was, resplendent in fluorescent lime green.

"What exactly did you sell?" Mrs. Flickinger asked in a trembling voice.

"Well..." he began, but he was interrupted.

Mr. Flickinger's voice rang out. "Ida! Ida, are you there?"

Mrs. Flickinger hurried out the door, presumably so her husband would not see the room. Rebecca figured Mrs. Flickinger would need to break the news to him gently.

"What is it?" she asked him.

"Does anyone know why there is a white goat tied to the front gate? She's eaten most of the flowers and has started on the gate post."

Mrs. Flickinger clasped her head with both hands. "A goat?" she squeaked.

Rebecca was concerned Mrs. Flickinger might faint right on the spot. She took her by the arm. "Would you like to sit down again?"

Mrs. Flickinger did not appear to hear her. "Goat, a goat," she repeated.

"That was my idea too," Nash said in a chirpy voice. "You know how you're always saying people want to have the Amish experience?" He looked up expectantly but was met with blank looks. He pushed on. "Well, I borrowed the goat. It gives the place a nice air of authenticity, don't you think?"

Mr. and Mrs. Flickinger continued to stare at Nash in shock. Rebecca was quite concerned for them. They did seem awfully distressed.

"And that's not all that's happened," Mr. Flickinger

continued. “The goat is the least of our problems. Henry is missing.”

Mrs. Flickinger gasped. “Did somebody leave the gate open?”

“No, it was shut. I’ve looked everywhere, but I can’t find him,” Mr. Flickinger said.

It was then Rebecca remembered she had seen Nash leading the horse down the road.

Suddenly Nash blurted out, “I sold him! Mom said I could.”

Mrs. Flickinger gasped. “I said no such thing!”

Nash appeared to be confused. He frowned so hard, his eyebrows formed a unibrow. “But I asked you if I could sell something you didn’t really need to fund the redecorating of the sitting room.”

“But we need our buggy horse of course!” Mrs. Flickinger said. It was the first time Rebecca had ever heard her raise her voice.

“You didn’t actually sell our buggy horse, did you?” Mr. Flickinger said. His face had gone as white as a sheet. “Is this a joke?”

“You don’t need a buggy horse,” Nash protested, “and the redecorating will bring in more business. The guests will love that room. It’s different.”

That’s an understatement, Rebecca thought.

Nash pushed on. “I can drive you anywhere you want in my car. Think of me as your own personal driver. I’ve saved you a lot of money, because you won’t have to feed that horse and you’ll get everywhere faster.”

Mr. and Mrs. Flickinger clutched each other, looking in horror at their son.

"Maybe we can buy him back," Mr. Flickinger said. "Who did you sell him to?"

Nash looked entirely smug. "I've done an extra good turn. When I was at the Millers' for dinner, I heard that Mrs. Ramseyer doesn't have a buggy horse any more. I sold her your horse cheap. She was ever so excited! She couldn't stop thanking me. And I can tell you, I spent every last cent of that money on your sitting room. I didn't even pay off any of my gambling debts, and I didn't gamble any of the money." Nash looked awfully self-satisfied and pleased with himself.

Rebecca could not believe she was hearing this. She thought perhaps she must be having a terrible dream and she was unable to awaken.

Mr. Flickinger seemed to be having trouble putting the pieces together. He took off his hat and scratched his head before putting his hat back on. "Let me see," he said in an even tone. "You sold our buggy horse to the Widow Ramseyer at a very cheap price?" Nash nodded. Mr. Flickinger continued. "You spent all the money Mrs. Ramseyer gave you on redecorating the sitting room. Is that right?"

Nash nodded again. "Yes, every last cent."

"Well then, you had better let me see the sitting room," Mr. Flickinger said. Nash and Mr. Flickinger headed for the room. Rebecca heard a loud gasp and then silence.

Mrs. Flickinger took her arm. "I need some meadow tea and whoopie pies." She clutched Rebecca's arm for support.

Rebecca helped Mrs. Flickinger into the kitchen and

made her some meadow tea and placed several whoopie pies in front of her. She figured Mrs. Flickinger was in shock and so would need the sugar.

"Do you think you can buy your horse back from Mrs. Ramseyer?" she asked Mrs. Flickinger.

Mr. Flickinger shook her head. "*Nee*, Rhoda needs that horse. Henry is a good reliable horse. *Gott* works in mysterious ways, and maybe this is *Gott's* way of providing Rhoda with a safe, reliable horse."

"What will you do for a buggy horse?" Rebecca asked her.

Mrs. Flickinger put her head in her hands and rested her elbows on the table. "We've put all our money into the B&B. There's no spare money for a horse, not a good one at any rate."

"We must tell the bishop," Rebecca said. "The bishop will know what to do. He'll make sure you get a good horse."

Nash was highly offended. He had decided to turn over a new leaf and be good, but no one appreciated all his hard work. He thought it was very enterprising of him to sell his parents' buggy horse to that widow. She was very excited about it and had given him lots of food to eat, so much in fact, that he hadn't even needed to stuff any in his pockets for later. He rubbed his stomach appreciatively. Why, he had never been given so much food at once.

And he hadn't spent the money on his gambling debts either. The old Nash would have done that. But no, he didn't even keep a cent for himself, and what gratitude was he shown for that? None! His parents weren't the slightest bit grateful that he hadn't kept the money for himself. Sometimes there was just no understanding people.

He hadn't expected his parents to like what he did. After all, they had no taste—they were Amish. On the other hand, he had been English for some time and he had impeccable taste, if he did say so himself. It's just that his parents really seemed to hate it. He thought they were overreacting. After all, what would they know?

He was sure the guests would absolutely love that sitting room. He liked it and he was going to spend time in front of that big TV. It was the only TV in the whole B&B.

And his parents hadn't even thanked him. He just couldn't get over their rudeness. They hadn't thanked him for spending all that time decorating that room and they hadn't even thanked him for providing the Widow Ramseyer with a cheap horse.

He shook his head. What was the world coming to?

Chapter Sixteen

Rebecca, her *mudder*, and Sarah Beachy all sat in the bishop's living room, chatting to the bishop's talkative wife, Fannie. Mrs. Miller had driven the *familye* buggy there on the pretext of telling the bishop about the Flickingers needing a new buggy horse, but Rebecca knew full well that her *mudder* was there for one reason, and one reason only, to find out all she could about Benjamin Shetler. Mrs. Miller was not a gossip, but the one thing she could not abide was having information kept from her.

By contrast, Mrs. Fannie Graber had a reputation in the community for not being able to keep a secret, and everyone suspected that her husband, the bishop, kept most things from her. Nevertheless, she did appear to have a far deeper knowledge about the goings-on in the community than any other person.

"I had just made a pot of bone set tea when you arrived," Fannie said. "It will go nicely with the whoopie pies. My husband will be home soon."

Rebecca was a little concerned. The bishop's wife fancied herself as a healer, and was always mixing up a concoction of herbs and serving them to people as tea. Most of them tasted downright awful.

Fannie poured everyone a cup of hot tea, and then looked expectantly at them while they tasted it. Rebecca took one sip, at the same time as Mrs. Miller said, "*Denki*, Fannie. I'll just wait for mine to cool down."

Why didn't I think of that? Rebecca asked herself. Aloud she said, "Oh it tastes unusual. What's in it?"

Fannie smiled. "It is a mixture of comfrey, wormwood, mallow, and horsetail."

"Isn't wormwood poisonous?" Rebecca asked, while wincing at the glare directed at her by her *mudder*.

Fannie shrugged. "There's only a little wormwood in the tea."

Rebecca forced a smile. The tea tasted dreadful, but she felt she needed to drink it so as not to offend the bishop's wife. She wished the weather was warmer, so they could sit outside and she tip the dreadful brew into the garden when Fannie Graber wasn't looking.

"Here is my husband now," Fannie Graber announced. She need not have said so; the bishop was walking into the room.

The bishop greeted everyone warmly. "Does someone wish to speak with me in private? What about you, Rachel?"

She waved one hand at him. "*Nee, denki.* I just came to mention the situation with the Flickingers' buggy horse."

"I'll fix you some bone set tea and something to eat," his wife said, but the bishop was fast to decline her offer.

"*Denki*, Fannie, but I have just eaten a large lunch at the Hershbergers' farm." He patted his stomach and laughed. "So what is this about the buggy horse?"

"I will leave it to Rebecca to explain," Mrs. Miller said, nodding to Rebecca.

Rebecca did not like being put on the spot. She was always anxious when people asked her to tell them something. She didn't know why, exactly, but she had been like that since childhood. She figured it probably stemmed from the time when their usual teacher was sick. The replacement teacher had been rather snappy to everyone, particularly Rebecca. She had barked questions at Rebecca, and if Rebecca hadn't responded instantly, the teacher became visibly angry.

Rebecca bit her lip. She didn't want to get Nash into trouble, but she couldn't see how she could avoid it. She took a deep breath and decided to tell it just the way it was. "It's a bit of a long story," she began, "but Nash, I mean Eli, told his parents he wanted to help with the bed and breakfast. He wanted to redecorate one of the sitting rooms, so Mrs. Flickinger told him there was paint in the barn."

Fannie interrupted her. "And did he use the paint in the barn?"

"*Nee*, he bought paint. But that's not all. He painted the walls dark purple and the ceiling black."

A collective gasp went up around the room. Rebecca saw her mother's jaw working furiously. "And there were three pieces of furniture already in the room. He painted those fluorescent green. He also bought a large flat-screen television."

"I can't see the relevance," Mrs. Miller snapped, "and why didn't you tell me about all this before, Rebecca? You take after your father. You and your father never tell me anything. I'm always the last to know." She shot Rebecca a sullen look.

Rebecca took another deep breath. "The relevance is that Nash had asked his mother if he could sell something so she wouldn't need to pay for the redecorating, and she agreed. I was there when he asked Mrs. Flickinger, and he was leaning on a chest of drawers. Anyway, he sold the buggy horse."

Fannie Graber gasped, but the bishop's expression remained impassive. Rebecca thought he had remarkable self-control and then figured he had probably heard worse in his lifetime. She pushed on. "The Flickingers didn't know he had sold their buggy horse until Mr. Flickinger couldn't find the horse in the field. Anyway, it turns out that Nash, I mean Eli, had dinner at our *haus* only the other night. My *vadder* said Mrs. Ramseyer's buggy horse had gone lame and she couldn't afford to buy a good reliable new horse. Nash said he was doing Mrs. Ramseyer a favor by selling her the horse very cheaply."

"Rebecca, you could have said all that in fewer words," Mrs. Miller said with a deep frown. "I will explain for you. The whole point of what Rebecca was trying to say is that Rhoda Ramseyer now has a cheap and good buggy horse, so the Flickingers do not want to take the horse back from her. They said she is welcome to keep the horse. Of course, the problem now remains that Samuel and Ida don't have a buggy horse. They don't have any money at all to buy another buggy horse, because they have put all their finances into their bed and breakfast business."

The bishop nodded. "I see. Well, we will have to take up a free will offering. Someone will have to go to the auctions and buy them a good horse. I know, Elijah is one of the most knowledgeable people with horses. Perhaps he and Samuel can go to the auctions together and select a horse."

Rebecca was at once relieved. "What can we do to help?" she asked the bishop.

"I will have to consult the ministers and the deacons, but since Samuel and Ida don't have a buggy horse, the need is rather urgent. We'll need to arrange a free will offering, or perhaps we should organize the community to sell pies door to door."

"Samuel and Ida will be pleased to hear that," Mrs. Miller said. "I do believe their son offered to drive them in his car, but I don't think they wished to accompany him anywhere."

The bishop nodded slowly. "Quite so, quite so." He looked at Rebecca. "We should be able to organize this fairly soon, and then you, Elijah and the Flickingers can go to the auctions and buy a good horse."

Rebecca shifted nervously on her feet. Why did the bishop assume she would too? Was it simply because she worked at the B&B, or was it because of Elijah? She narrowed her eyes and stared at the bishop. He did look quite pleased with himself.

Fannie turned to her husband. "Do we know anyone who has a good buggy horse for sale?"

"*Nee*, I don't know of anyone with a suitable horse for sale," he told her. "I know of several young horses for sale, but they are not suitable. No, I am certain they will need to buy a horse from an auction."

"I hope a suitable horse will be found," Mrs. Miller said.

"I'm sure a suitable horse can be found at the auctions," the bishop said. "I know there is a horse auction at the end of the week. Gideon Lapp is selling his Dutch Warmblood stallion there. I'll ask him if he's heard of any good horses being sold. Perhaps he could recommend one."

"Those poor people," Fannie said. "I must bake them a lime and sardine cream pie."

With that, the bishop stood up. "I will go and ask Gideon Lapp now," he said.

"Aren't you going to have something to eat?" his wife urged him.

"I would like to, but this is an urgent matter." The bishop disappeared out the door.

Rebecca bit back a smile. She knew the bishop must be getting his food from somewhere else, because he could hardly live on Fannie's unique offerings. Rebecca had noticed that on the occasions the bishop had visited the Millers, he had always eaten a considerable amount.

After the bishop left, Fannie turned her attention to Sarah, who was already fidgeting nervously. "Do you like living in these parts, Sarah?"

"Oh yes, *denki*, Mrs. Graber."

Fannie sipped some bone set tea before speaking again. "Do you think you will stay here long?" She shot a long, penetrating look at Sarah, a fact which did not go unmissed by Rebecca.

Hmm, Mrs. Graber knows something about Sarah that I don't know, she thought.

Sarah twisted her apron in her hands. "*Jah*, so long as Mrs. Miller will have me."

"You are welcome to stay as long as you like, Sarah."

"*Denki*, Mrs. Miller."

Mrs. Miller turned her tea cup around, but did not pick it up. "There have been several new people arrive in our community lately, haven't there, Fannie."

Mrs. Graber set her tea cup down. "*Jah*, that there have been. Sarah, the Flickingers, their son, Eli, and now Benjamin Shetler."

"Oh, I meant new people who will be staying in the community for some time, not just passing guests." Mrs. Miller narrowed her eyes, and Rebecca could see that this was part of her *mudder's* plan to extract information from Fannie Graber.

Fannie did not take the bait, but merely asked, "What do you mean?"

Mrs. Miller looked a little exasperated. "Benjamin Shetler is only a guest at the B&B. He hasn't moved into the community."

"Oh, he'll be here quite some time." Fannie Graber smiled to herself, and Rebecca could see that she was enjoying some private knowledge.

Rebecca was so intent watching the exchange between her *mudder* and Fannie that she had not noticed

Sarah's reaction, but clearly her *mudder* had. "Sarah, are you all right? You look quite ill," Mrs. Miller said.

Sarah had gone white again. "I just feel a bit dizzy."

Fannie's hand flew to her mouth. "Oh, I'm so sorry, Sarah. Drink the tea; it will help you feel better."

Rebecca and her *mudder* exchanged glances. Why did Fannie apologize to Sarah? Was Sarah connected in some way with Benjamin Shetler?

Clearly exasperated, Mrs. Miller tried the straight-forward approach and addressed Fannie Graber directly. "Do you know why Benjamin Shetler is here?"

Rebecca had to hide her gasp by pretending to cough. She had never heard her *mudder* being so blunt in trying to extract information from somebody. Her gaze turned to Fannie.

Fannie laughed and her eyes settled on her tea, rather than on Mrs. Miller. "Oh, goodness me. I don't know too much about the goings-on around here. People come and go all the time."

Rebecca knew that was not the case. There wasn't very much in the way of coming and goings at all, and never anything like this. It seemed quite clear from Fannie's reaction that there was definitely something going on that she was not at liberty to disclose. Rebecca unconsciously tapped on her chin as she wondered what it could be.

Sarah shifted uncomfortably in her seat, before she said, "It's very cold for this time of year, isn't it?"

Fannie was quick to accept the change in the conversation. "*Jah*, it is. I was just thinking that this morning as I pinned out the washing." Fannie took another sip of tea, placed it back on the saucer, and smiled widely. *A little too widely*, Rebecca thought.

Mrs. Miller, undaunted, pushed on. "Someone said that Benjamin was taken to the B&B by Mr. Graber, so you'd know a little something about him, wouldn't you?"

Fannie fixed her eyes on Mrs. Miller and then shot a glance at Sarah, before saying, "He very well could have been. Mr. Graber entertains visitors all the time, and often I don't get to see who they are at all." Fannie finished off with a flourish of her hand and a giggle.

The statement did not ring true to Rebecca, and by the look on her *mudder's* face, it seemed clear that she too realized that they were not going to get any information from Fannie. It was as if Fannie had suddenly become tight lipped. She was usually much easier to get information from. There was clearly something going on.

"Are you feeling better, dear?" Fannie asked Sarah.

Sarah nodded. "*Jah, denki*."

"I had just made a tray of sandwiches just before you visited," Fannie said. "I'll fetch them. Sarah, you probably have forgotten to eat, haven't you?"

Sarah smiled weakly, and before long, Fannie returned with a tray of sandwiches, all cut into triangles, which she placed on the table. "Here, Sarah, eat this one." Fannie held out the tray to Sarah, and then to Mrs. Miller, and finally, to Rebecca. They all dutifully took a sandwich and put it on their plates. Rebecca wished she had pockets so she could stuff the sandwich into them to avoid having to eat it.

"Now, Sarah, eat that sandwich. It will make you feel better."

Sarah took a mouthful and at once looked as if she was going to be violently ill. She reached for the bone seat tea and took a gulp, while tears ran down her face. "What's in the sandwich?" she finally managed to ask.

"Wasabi on canned eel," Fannie said. "It's a bit hot, but you get used to it. I should have told you to eat it slowly."

Rebecca and Mrs. Miller exchanged glances. "How inventive, Fannie," Mrs. Miller said politely. "And what's in these sandwiches that Rebecca and I have?"

Fannie leaned over and peeled each sandwich open to look inside. "Yours is hazelnut-chocolate spread on anchovies, and Rebecca's is thin slices of raw liver with soft cod roe and parsley. It's very good for you, full of iron and vitamin C."

"Perhaps you could take a plate of sandwiches to Benjamin Shetler," Mrs. Miller said, and Rebecca could not help but admire the way in which her *mudder* had brought the *mann* in question back into the conversation. "It must be hard for him not knowing anyone in the community."

"I didn't say he didn't know anyone in the community," Fannie said smugly, looking directly at Sarah before while helping herself to one of her sandwiches.

Rebecca studied her *mudder* who sat primly with a straight back and her hands clutched tightly together in her lap. In her *mudder's* eyes was a determination to get to the bottom of the Benjamin Shetler story, but Fannie was being uncharacteristically less than forthcoming.

And why did Fannie Graber look at Sarah like that when she answered Mamm? Rebecca wondered. There was definitely something fishy going on, and it wasn't just the sandwiches.

Chapter Seventeen

Mrs. Flickinger was the only woman in the community who had not been frantically making all manner of pies for the fundraiser. The bishop, the ministers, and the deacons did not think it proper that the Ida Flickinger should contribute to the purchase price of her new buggy horse, given that everyone else was raising the money for them for the horse. However, Mrs. Flickinger had told Rebecca to go home early so she could help her mother, Mary, and Sarah.

Everyone had been busy taking orders from the entire community. Yard signs had been put up, and local stores had been notified. There were plenty of orders and lots of pies to make.

Rebecca was in her mother's kitchen making a layered dessert with pineapple, peaches, and Jell-O. Sarah and Mary were making banana puddings and cracker puddings.

"Do you think we will raise enough money for a horse?" Rebecca asked her mother.

"Yes, there will certainly be enough money for a horse. The only question is, what sort of horse will it be? Some horses appear fine, but they have had old injuries, or they have bad tempers through previous ill-treatment by people. You don't really know what you're getting when you buy a horse from an auction. I've never approved of buying a horse from an auction."

Rebecca remembered how many times her mother had complained about buying horses from an auction. Mrs. Miller was still speaking. "I know many other people, even the bishop, who have bought horses from an auction, and they have been very satisfied with the horses, but when I was a young girl, my parents bought a horse from an auction. He trotted well, and the auctioneer said he was well broke and he said traffic didn't worry him. When that horse met his first truck, he took off. It was all my father could do to hold him. Eventually, we sold him to *Englischers* as a show horse. He was certainly not good as a buggy horse."

"What breed of horse was he?" Sarah asked her.

Mrs. Miller pulled a face. "I don't know what the English call them. They are some sort of fancy high-stepping horse. They look good, sure, but they can't work pulling a buggy."

Rebecca had heard that story many times before. "I do hope the Flickingers get a safe, reliable horse," she said. "What a shame one of our neighbors doesn't have one for sale."

Mrs. Miller waved her finger at her. "*Jah*, that would be the best course of action, to buy a horse from people we know. Still, people from other communities will be there selling horses, and they can give you the background history on the horse."

"Are you going to the auction?" Mary asked Rebecca.

Mrs. Miller answered for Rebecca. "Yes, she's going with Samuel and Ida Flickinger. The bishop suggested they take Elijah with them because he's a good judge of horses."

Both Sarah and Mary smiled at Rebecca. *No doubt they think there's something going on*, Rebecca thought. She avoided their gaze and changed the subject.

"I certainly hope we make enough money for a reliable horse, then," Rebecca said, returning to her earlier sentiment. "Do old reliable horses fetch more money than fast younger horses?"

Mrs. Miller paused, a rolling pin in her hand. "I don't believe they do," she said, wiping flour from her face, but actually dabbing more on in the process. "I would think a fast young horse would bring more money than an old, safe, reliable horse, especially if that horse is ugly."

Mary gasped. "Mrs. Miller, horses aren't ugly."

Mrs. Miller smiled weakly. "*Nee*, I meant the horse might have old injuries and scars. Even though such things don't affect the horse, they will make the horse bring a lower price. Elijah might be able to find a bargain in a horse of that type."

Rebecca was surprised that her mother was praising Elijah. Still, Elijah's three *bruders* were married to Rebecca's *schweschders*, and Mrs. Miller had shown no resentment to Katie Hostetler for some time now. Rebecca figured that her mother had forgiven Noah for causing the buggy accident. Of course, everyone knew it wasn't his fault, but her mother was known to hold grudges. Still, the three marriages and the birth of three *bopplin* seemed to have washed all the resentment away.

Or had it? Mrs. Miller was an avid matchmaker, and she had not once tried to match Rebecca with Elijah. Rebecca rubbed her chin. On the other hand, her mother hadn't really tried to match her with anyone else. She wondered why.

"As soon as these pies are baked, we need to start delivering them," Mrs. Miller said. "Rebecca, do you have the list?"

Rebecca looked at her mother blankly. "What list?"

Her mother shook her head. "No matter. I forgot Katie Hostetler has the list. We'll have to drive there with our pies and collect her pies."

Perhaps the rift between the two familyes has been well and truly mended, after all, Rebecca thought.

After the pies were baked, the women cleaned the kitchen. There was quite some cleaning to do. They then changed into fresh clothes and assembled in the living room. "Now take those pies out to the buggy very carefully," Mrs. Miller said. "We don't want any accidents. If one of you were to trip over a stone, you could undo hours of work."

Rebecca made her way gingerly to the buggy. It took them several trips, but soon the buggy was laden with pies. "I'll drive you to Mrs. Hostetler's now," Mrs. Miller said. "Well, don't stand there looking vacant. Let's go!"

Rebecca's heart was in her mouth with the prospect

she might see Elijah. Then again she might not—he could be out in the fields or attending to a fence on the other side of the farm. However, he walked out of the house as soon as Mrs. Miller brought the buggy to a stop.

"*Hullo*, Mrs. Miller. *Hiya*, Rebecca, Sarah, and Mary."

Everyone greeted him in return. Mrs. Hostetler hurried down the steps behind him. "I think it will have too many pies, Rachel. Anna Hershberger, Susan Lapp, and Bertha King have brought their pies here. It's too many for the one buggy. Elijah said he'd help, so Elijah and I will go in our buggy. We have room for one more person," she said.

Mrs. Miller hesitated, but Mary said in a loud voice, "Why don't you go, Rebecca. Sarah and I will help Mrs. Miller."

Rebecca's cheeks burned. She hoped Elijah didn't think Mary was trying to matchmake the two of them. Still, she thought Katie Hostetler looked mighty pleased and wondered if she had planned this all the time. She knew Mrs. Hostetler wanted her to marry Elijah. She had made no secret of the fact.

Elijah held out his hand and helped Rebecca into the buggy. "Now you two *youngie* chat and I'll drive," Mrs. Hostetler said.

Rebecca thought that was far from subtle and her cheeks continued to burn. Elijah, however, didn't seem to mind. "I'm hoping there will be enough money raised to be able to buy a really good horse for the Flickingers," he said. "I feel so sorry for them with their buggy horse being sold like that. Still, I suppose Nash was trying to help."

"Who would know?" Rebecca said, and Elijah shot her a sharp look. She added, "The Flickingers need a steady safe horse, not a fast horse, as you know. Does that sort of horse often come up for sale at an auction?"

Elijah nodded. "Yes, there are often several of them."

"*Mamm* said there might be a horse that didn't look good, because it was covered in scars or something like that, and *Mamm* said the horse would bring a lower price."

Elijah was quick to agree. "Yes, the Flickingers don't care what the horse looks like and they don't want a fast horse. The horse that Nash sold Mrs. Ramseyer was an old plodding type of horse, not a young, fast horse. It's the young, fast horses that bring the big money at auction."

Rebecca breathed a sigh of relief. "So you do think we will raise enough money?"

"Of course we will," Elijah said confidently. "And even if there is a shortfall, then the bishop will take up a free will offering."

Rebecca's spirits lifted. "Of course. Why, I knew that."

She saw Katie watching them out of the corner of her eye, so she shifted uneasily on the bench seat.

The first house was that of *Englischers*. They had ordered five apple pies. Mrs. Hostetler said she would stay in the buggy and asked Elijah and Rebecca to deliver the pies. Elijah took three pies, leaving Rebecca to carry two. "Can you manage?" he asked, concern in his voice.

"*Jah, denki*," Rebecca said.

The English lady who met him at the door was delighted to have the pies, and handed over extra money. "Amish make the best pies," she said. "Did you make them yourselves?"

Rebecca chuckled. "No several people in the community made these."

"Well, thanks again," the lady said. "You two make such a lovely couple."

Elijah shot Rebecca a look, but she could meet not his eyes. Why had the lady said such a thing? Did they look like a couple? Perhaps the lady simply assumed that an Amish woman and Amish man together in public were married or dating. Rebecca nodded slowly to herself. Yes, that must be it. That must have been what she thought.

Rebecca thought back to when she had seen an English man and an English woman together. She always assumed they were a couple, but maybe they were just good friends or maybe even brother and sister. Yes, it was human nature to jump to conclusions.

That was, of course, unless the lady had sensed Rebecca's attraction to Elijah. Or was Elijah attracted to her? Or was the fact that he knew his mother wanted him to marry Rebecca firmly on his mind? For years everyone had assumed that Rebecca and Elijah would marry. Maybe Elijah was moving mindlessly in that direction.

Rebecca didn't want that. She wanted love, true love.

The ministers always said that *Gott* has appointed one woman for a man and one man for every woman. That is what Rebecca wanted, true love, and not just a marriage of convenience or a marriage because people expected it of them.

"Are Martha and Moses enjoying visiting?" Katie asked Rebecca.

"Yes, they are enjoying visiting very much," Rebecca said.

"And how is Mrs. Flickinger's son enjoying his visit?"

"I don't think he's enjoying it at all, to be honest," Rebecca said with a chuckle. "I think he is quite bored."

"Why did he go back to live with his parents if he is bored?" Elijah asked, furrowing his brow.

"I think he simply ran out of money," Rebecca said. Nash had told her that he had run up huge gambling debts, but it wasn't her place to repeat it.

Mrs. Hostetler drove all over the community to Amish houses, as well as to English houses. It took hours for them to deliver all the pies. After they had delivered the last pie and Mrs. Hostetler had turned the horse for home, she said, "You two work well together. You make a good couple."

Elijah looked down at his feet and Rebecca was discomfited. Finally, Elijah spoke. "*Mamm's* turned into a matchmaker," he said.

Rebecca laughed, although she was awfully self-conscious. "She's not as bad as my *mudder*." They both spoke in low tones, and Mrs. Hostetler was acting if she couldn't hear them. Whether she could not, Rebecca didn't know.

"I have forgotten to give my mother the list of why we shouldn't be married," Elijah said with a chuckle.

"Oh yes, we should send it to *The Diary* newspaper and ask them to publish it," Rebecca said, "because then everyone will leave us alone."

"There is another way to get them to leave us alone," Elijah said.

Rebecca looked at him with interest. "What is it?"

"We could get married," Elijah said with a wink. "If we were married, people would stop bothering us to get married, wouldn't they? It's quite logical."

"It is logical indeed," Rebecca said, forcing a laugh. She and Elijah used to joke about such things, but she didn't want to be hurt. She was hopelessly in love with Elijah and she could see for herself that his mother was making it quite plain that she wanted Elijah to marry her. And while the two of them were good friends, Elijah only spoke about their relationship in joking terms.

Rebecca was concerned. Maybe Elijah wanted to marry her in the hopes that love would come later. Why, Mrs. Miller had told her other daughters that love would come later when she was trying to matchmake them with someone unsuitable. Rebecca wondered if that was Elijah's belief as well. Did he really think love would come later?

Rebecca shook her head to clear her thoughts. Where was she going with this line of thought? Elijah hadn't even asked her to marry him, and already she was examining his motivations for doing so.

Still, what would she say if he did? She could hardly

refuse, feeling about him the way she did. But could she live in a loveless marriage?

Rebecca's spirits sank as Katie Hostetler happily chatted away to her and the sun disappeared over the rolling hills.

Chapter Eighteen

Rebecca was on her way to the horse auction with the Flickingers and Elijah. However, Nash had insisted on accompanying them. He said it was his fault he had sold the horse to Mrs. Ramseyer, so the least he could do was to help choose a horse.

The Flickingers had not seemed pleased with the news. Rebecca could plainly see Elijah was not happy about Nash accompanying them either.

"Your horse is fast," Nash said to Elijah. "I've seen another black horse around here."

"That must be Jessie Yoder's horse," Rebecca said, thinking of the tall, flashy, high-stepping horse Jessie Yoder drove around. The horse had a reputation, and Jessie was one of the few people who could handle him. Clearly she shared her brother, David's, love for animals and was good with them. *It's a shame she doesn't extend that same kindness to people*, Rebecca thought, and then silently chastized herself for being so unkind.

Nash chatted all the way to the auction. "I haven't

been any distance in a buggy for ages," he said. "I'd forgotten how slow and useless they are."

Rebecca gasped. Nash certainly didn't have a filter. He just said what he thought and he didn't care how it impacted others.

She saw Mr. and Mrs. Flickinger exchange glances.

When they got to the auction, Elijah tied up his horse. A Mennonite man at once approached him. "Is this horse in the auction?"

"*Nee*, not at all," Elijah said. "I'm just here to help a friend buy a horse. I'm not selling my horse."

The man shot Elijah's horse an appraising look before walking away.

Rebecca saw Nash staring after the man, and for a moment she was worried that Nash would sell Elijah's horse without his permission. When Mr. and Mrs. Flickinger walked off in the direction of the barn, Rebecca tugged on Elijah's arm. "You will think I'm quite strange, but I thought Nash was watching that man walk away from you—you know, the man who asked if your horse was for sale. I know it sounds crazy, but what if he tries to sell your horse to the man? I think Nash would like to have some money of his own." As soon as she said it, Rebecca felt quite silly foolish. "I forget I said anything," she said with a nervous laugh.

Elijah leaned forward, so close she could smell his fragrance of hay and handmade oatmeal soap. "I'm thinking exactly the same thing," he said. "I'm going to keep an eye on Nash. I'm not going to let him out of my sight."

"Good idea," Rebecca said. She considered how easy

the conversation was and how well the two of them got along with each other. Yet she wanted more than friendship—she wanted love, a deep abiding, romantic love. She knew some people in the community had married and said love would come later, and she had no idea whether it had or it hadn't. Maybe they were in love now and maybe they weren't. One thing was certain, Rebecca had decided she would only marry if she was in love, and the man was in love with her. She couldn't abide the thought of a loveless marriage.

Mr. and Mrs. Flickinger were waiting for them outside the big barn. "Samuel and I will inspect some horses now," Elijah said. "Would you like to come with us, Nash?"

Nash looked mighty pleased, but Rebecca knew Elijah had invited him so he could keep an eye on him. Mrs. Flickinger tapped her arm. "Come, Rebecca, let us get good seats now."

As they entered the barn, Esther was surprised to see it was almost filled. However, there was a vacant row at the front. "Let's spread out," Mrs. Flickinger said, "so there's room for three more."

Rebecca sat in the front row. There were five sets of seats behind her and the room was alive with excitement. One of the spotters for the auctioneer stood in front of her so she had to crane her neck to see what was going on. She was diagonally opposite the auctioneer and the person writing for him. Several bottles of water sat on the desk in front of them.

Rebecca and Mrs. Flickinger ended up setting a fair way apart. Mrs. Flickinger deposited a large tote bag in the middle of the space between them to dissuade anyone who might attempt to sit there.

It seemed like an age before the men returned, and Rebecca wished she had gone to see the horses too. Still, she knew it was important to get good seats.

When the men returned, Mr. Hostetler sat next to Mrs. Hostetler, and Elijah moved to set next to Esther, but Nash pushed past him and sat so close to Rebecca that it made her uncomfortable, and she moved a little away from him. She leaned around Nash and addressed Elijah, who looked rather put out. "Did you find any suitable horses?"

"Yes, we were particularly taken with a nice bay," Elijah said. "He's twelve and he's a Standardbred. He raced as a three-year-old, but had shin splints so he's been used as a buggy horse ever since."

"Is he a nice horse?" Rebecca asked.

Nash made a sound of disgust. "No, he's even uglier than the last horse. He doesn't look fast at all. Now there was a very pretty black horse there that I really liked. If I was an Amish person, that's the sort of horse I'd be going for."

Elijah frowned. "The horse has a very good temperament and is sound. He's had some knocks and bumps over the years, but he comes with a veterinary certificate of soundness."

"Why is his owner selling him?" Rebecca asked.

Nash interrupted. "That's a very good question, Rebecca. I'm glad to see you have a suspicious mind and you're not gullible. Yes, that's exactly what I wondered. Why are all these people selling their horses? I can understand the breeders selling the young ones, but there must be something wrong for someone to sell a horse."

"Not at all," Elijah said. "Sometimes they might find the horse is too slow for them or maybe even too fast. Maybe the *familye's* current horses have taken a dislike to the new horse. There could be any number of genuine reasons."

"Well, you sure are more trusting than I am," Nash said with another snort.

Elijah shook his head. "The seller's father owned the horse, but he went to be with *Gott.* The son had no need of another buggy horse, and that is why he is selling the horse today. Samuel thinks this horse will be as reliable as Henry," Elijah continued. "There were a few other people looking at him, that's the only problem."

Rebecca whispered, "Do you think there's enough money to buy him?"

"Nothing is ever certain, but I'm fairly confident," Elijah said.

Although the Amish did not like to be prideful, Rebecca was proud of Elijah for helping the Flickingers select the horse and for the fact the bishop had entrusted him with the money from the fundraiser to make the buying decision. *He'd make a good father*, she thought, and then wondered why she had thought such a thing. *It's a horse auction*, she silently berated herself.

Elijah leaned over Nash once more and spoke to Rebecca. "This horse is on toward the end of the sale."

"I hope everyone's run out of money by then," Rebecca said with a laugh.

"I still don't like that horse," Nash complained.

"There were much nicer horses out there and they were much faster too."

"But Samuel and Ida want a slow, reliable horse, not a fast horse," Elijah said.

"Typical," Nash said. He crossed his arms over his chest.

Rebecca had never been to a buggy horse auction so watched everything with interest. The first horse was driven in. Rebecca had expected that the horse would be led around but she was shocked that the horse was driven through the center of the barn and at that, driven very quickly. Another horse appeared soon after. Rebecca did a double take and realized it was the same horse.

A young Amish woman drove a tall bay horse through the centre of the barn quickly. The woman was leaning back, hanging onto the horse with all her might. Rebecca wondered why anyone would need a horse as fast as that. She certainly wouldn't like to drive such a fast horse. He certainly didn't look reliable, and if there's one thing an Amish buggy horse needed to be, it was reliable and safe with traffic.

The horse was sold rather quickly and the next horse came in. This horse too was driven through the barn at high speed. The man standing next to the auctioneer announced the horse was the Standardbred and that he was very fast and also safe to drive in traffic. "He's a well-broke horse," the man concluded.

That horse was sold for a high price. The next horse was led by a man who was running quite fast. The auctioneer's assistant said, "Very well mannered, started in harness, and shows a lot of potential. This horse is only two years old and he can really trot."

Rebecca was a little discouraged. These horses could all trot very fast and they were all beautiful horses, but Henry had been steady and reliable, not fancy and not fast. She was worried the Flickingers would not be able to buy a suitable horse at this auction.

The next horse was a tall, beautiful mare. The man announced, "This horse shows a lot of dressage potential if anyone is interested in that. She has a very nice canter too." As the horse was driven back through the barn in the other direction, the man added, "She does not have papers, but they are available and the seller will pay for her registration at his expense and mail them to the buyer."

Rebecca realized his comments were addressed to the *Englischers* in the barn, but she could not see any from where she was sitting.

Nash muttered as every horse entered, and commented loudly on each horse. Rebecca wished she could sit somewhere else. Presently, Mrs. Flickinger passed pieces of watermelon to them all. Nash offered his piece to Rebecca.

"Don't you like watermelon?" she asked him.

He pulled a face. "It's fine, but I want a burger or a steak. I haven't eaten since breakfast."

"None of us have," Rebecca pointed out.

"But I'm not Amish any more," he said.

Rebecca puzzled over that for several moments and still did not know what he meant.

Finally, the horse Elijah had selected was driven in.

"That's him," Elijah said.

Rebecca at once felt sorry for the horse. He was not thin, but he certainly could do with some more weight, and his coat was not at all shiny. She hoped they would buy the horse so she could take him carrots and groom him and make him happy again. Even when he was driven past she thought there was a sense of sadness about him.

The bidding was fast and furious to start with, and Elijah didn't bid. Rebecca wondered why, but she didn't want to distract him by asking. Just as the bidding died down, Elijah made a bid.

Someone countered and then Elijah immediately bid again.

It was all over. The horse was knocked down to Elijah.

"Elijah, that was excellent bidding," Samuel Flickinger said to Elijah. "You had me worried for a moment. Clearly, you're experienced at this."

"I'm glad you've got the horse," Elijah said. "Rebecca, would you like to come and see him now since you didn't see him before?"

Rebecca jumped to her feet, but Nash said, "Yes, I'd love to. Thanks, Elijah."

Rebecca considered telling Nash to stay behind, but she thought that would be rude. She had wanted to have some alone time with Elijah. Still, she knew Elijah didn't want to let Nash out of his sight so she thought maybe it was a good thing he was coming along.

They went out to the horse barn, carefully stepping under the rope of a horse cross-tied in the center. "Here he is," Elijah said.

"So you bought him, did you?" a man asked.

When Elijah nodded, he shook hands with Elijah. "This is Rebecca Miller, and Nash," Elijah said.

The man shook both their hands. "Will you be looking after him?" he said to Rebecca.

"Actually, he belongs to the people I work for," she said. "Their horse has, um, gone to a widow and so they needed this horse. They want a steady reliable horse."

"Peter is very reliable," the man who had introduced himself as John said. "Peter belonged to my father. Even when my father was feeble and ill, he drove him all the time. You won't get a more reliable horse."

Rebecca gently stroked the horse's face and then kissed him on the nose. To her surprise, Nash did too. She had forgotten for a moment that he loved animals.

"I thought you said he wasn't attractive," she said in low tones.

"Don't say that in front of the horse," Nash said.

Rebecca shot him a look. She had no idea whether or not he was joking.

"I suppose we're going home now," Nash said, "unless you're going to buy another horse?"

"Just the one horse," Elijah said.

Rebecca noted Elijah was tense around Nash.

Nash winked at Rebecca. "Well, Rebecca and I will look after this horse. You don't need to worry about that," he said to Elijah.

Elijah folded his arms and looked cross.

After smirking at Elijah, Nash wandered off to look at the other horses, much to Rebecca's relief.

"What do you think of him?" Elijah asked Rebecca.

"I love him; he's wonderful," Rebecca said. "His coat is a bit rough and he's a little on the thin side, don't you think?"

"Definitely," Elijah said, "but it won't take him long to blossom in your care, Rebecca."

Rebecca smiled. The pleasant moment was broken by Nash.

"You know, I'm almost disappointed I'm English now," he said. "There are a few horses here I'd like to buy. What a shame the Amish don't race their horses. Then we could bet on them and make some money."

Rebecca pulled a face. She thought she had better not comment. She caught Elijah's eye and he smiled at her.

Rebecca's heart melted. *If only Elijah was in love with me*, she lamented.

Chapter Nineteen

Nash congratulated himself on his plan. He knew that Mrs. Miller and Mary would be visiting the Yoders all day, and Rebecca was already at work at the B&B. He figured she wouldn't get through the huge pile of ironing he had told her Mrs. Flickinger insist she do at once. He had lied of course, but Rebecca wasn't likely to find out anytime soon. Martha and Moses were still away visiting, the greedy things, getting nice gifts from everyone they visited. *What a good way to score free stuff,* he thought. That meant that the blonde girl, Sarah, would be alone at the Miller *haus.*

Nash drove around the corner, more slowly than usual, so as not to dislodge the sugar cream pie he had just bought in town. It wouldn't do if it fell off the seat. He had borrowed a plate from the B&B when no one was looking, and had done everything he could to make the pie look homemade. He chuckled to himself as he drove. This was fun, the most fun he'd had in a long time.

He drove up slowly, cut the engine and let the car slide in. He had no wish to alert Mr. Miller to his presence.

Nash walked up to the door, sugar cream pie in hand. Light flakes of snow were starting to fall, and he pulled his coat around him, grateful that the coat covered all his tattoos. He had also removed all his piercings for the day. He knew that people judged him by how he looked, so he had done his best to look inoffensive and believable for once.

As soon as Sarah opened the door, Nash spoke, careful to speak in Pennsylvania Dutch. "*Hiya*, Sarah. My *mudder* sent this sugar cream pie over for the Millers. I wanted to apologize for my behavior at dinner the other night. Is Mrs. Miller home?" He put on his most hopeful expression.

"*Denki. Nee*, she isn't," Sarah said. "Won't you come in?" She stood aside and Nash walked inside the *haus*. He handed her the pie. She took it to the kitchen and then returned. "Would you like some meadow tea?"

Nash smiled broadly, and turned on the charm. "*Denki*. It's quite chilly." He paused for effect. "Yet we should sit outside on the porch to drink the tea, if it will not be too cold for you?"

Sarah nodded appreciatively. "I'll get my coat after I make the tea."

Nash walked outside to sit on the porch. He was quite pleased with himself, figuring that Sarah would consider he had good manners to suggest sitting outside the house. It was not the done thing in the community for an unmarried girl and an unmarried man to be alone in a house together, with no others present.

Nash looked out over the rolling fields and hills. *How could anyone live here?* he asked himself. *The most exciting thing in view is a cow. It's so boring, there's nothing to do. I can't believe these people actually live here.*

Yet Nash was feeling quite smug. Everything was falling into place nicely. He was so pleased with himself that he barely noticed Sarah return with two mugs of tea. He thanked her and wrapped his hands around his mug of tea to warm his hands.

"Are you on *rumspringa*?"

Nash looked at Sarah. "*Jah*. It's been a long *rumspringa*, and like many of the *youngie* on *rumspringa*, I did some foolish things. I confessed to the bishop in my own community, and then came on here to see if my *daed* and my *mudder* would forgive me." He wiped a pretend tear from his eye. "I won't return to the community until after they've forgiven me." Nash was satisfied to see the sympathy in Sarah's eyes.

"Oh, I'm so sorry."

Nash nodded. "I also wanted to see my *grossmammi* again with her being so old and frail, even if my parents had said I couldn't."

"Your parents said you couldn't see your *grossmammi*?"

She's hooked, Nash thought with satisfaction. Aloud he said, "*Jah*, sadly that is the case. The bishop from our community told them they had to allow me to come here, but they haven't forgiven me for the bad things I did on *rumspringa*."

"But you repented."

Nash just shrugged. "And then I thought I was helping Mrs. Ramseyer by selling her my parents' buggy horse cheap. I thought I could drive my parents everywhere in my car, and thought that would help them too. I had the best of intentions, but my plan backfired on me."

Sarah hurried to reassure him. "Your heart was in the right place."

"Anyway, I must apologize for calling in on you when you were alone." He fixed the most pious expression on his face that he could muster.

Sarah looked a little embarrassed and simply smiled shyly at him.

"I hope it doesn't cause problems between you and Elijah." Nash was careful to look out toward the rolling hills when he said that, but he could still see Sarah's reaction in his peripheral vision.

"Elijah? Whatever do you mean?"

Nash was concerned. Sarah actually appeared to be shocked. He didn't think a simple Amish girl would be such a good actor; it must be genuine. He now turned his full gaze upon Sarah. "Oh do forgive me if I've overstepped the mark. It's just that everyone thinks you and Elijah…well…" He let his words hang, and he looked at Sarah from under his long eyelashes.

"Oh no, you have it wrong," Sarah hastened to explain. "It's Rebecca and Elijah."

Nash thought for a moment how to play this. "Yes, I must have it wrong," he said. "But I heard my *mudder* and Rebecca talking in the kitchen, and Rebecca said that she no longer had feelings for Elijah. She said that a few weeks ago Elijah told her he liked another *maidel*. Rebecca told my *mudder* that she was upset at the time, but has moved on." Nash hoped that was believable; *he* wouldn't have believed the far-fetched story he had just invented on the spot, but then again, he wasn't a sweet and naïve young girl.

"I'm surprised Rebecca didn't say something to me," Sarah said.

Nash continued to look at Sarah and raised his eyebrows, waiting for her to make the connection. When, much to his annoyance, she didn't, he continued. "I could be wrong, but I thought the other *maidel* was you."

"Me?" To Nash's disappointment, Sarah looked alarmed. For his plan to work, Sarah would need to have at least a little crush on Elijah. It didn't seem that this was the case.

"It's not my place to say," Nash said, injecting concern into his voice. "I shouldn't have repeated what I'd heard." He sipped his tea, hoping Sarah would say something. He was not disappointed.

"I have no idea about Elijah, but I know he's not interested in me," Sarah said thoughtfully. "As for how Rebecca feels about him, I don't know."

Nash's plan had gone out the window, so he said the first thing that came into his head. "The new *mann* at the B&B asked Rebecca on a buggy ride."

Sarah knocked her tea over, at the same time exclaiming, "Benjamin Shetler?"

Nash hurried to right the mug. He was now in high spirits again. Why would Sarah care if Benjamin Shetler and Rebecca Miller were dating? Yet clearly she did. This was a new twist. His plan wasn't a failure, after all.

Chapter Twenty

Rebecca pulled on her black coat, fastened it, and headed out the door of the B&B. She only remembered just half an hour earlier that she had offered to help Hannah with the twins so that Hannah could have a well-earned rest. She hurried to Hannah's *haus*. It was a little way over the rise in the hill and if it had been any further it would have been too far to walk in the cold weather.

Although she was tired, Rebecca knew that Hannah would have been even more so with looking after the twins all day and all night, especially now that they were teething.

She could hear the twins' cries as she hurried up to the *haus*. "Hello, I'm here," she called as she pushed the door open.

Hannah's face was filled with relief. "I'm so pleased you didn't forget to come."

"Of course I wouldn't forget. I've been looking forward to it all day." Rebecca sent up a silent prayer to *Gott* to forgive her for the white lie.

Hannah had Mason on her hip. He was dribbling and crying and had poked a finger in his mouth. Rebecca could see Rose in the wooden playpen in the corner of the room.

"Give him to me." Rebecca put her arms out. Mason put an arm out to her and she took him from Hannah.

Hannah rubbed her eyes. "I can't thank you enough for this, Rebecca. I'm so looking forward to having a sleep. I haven't slept a wink in the last two days. Well, perhaps I slept for an hour or two, I'm too tired to remember." Her voice was slurred.

"You go upstairs now. I'll stay until you wake up."

As Hannah was walking upstairs, Rebecca wondered what was going to happen with dinner. She guessed she would have to cook that too, as well as look after the crying twins. "Hannah, what about dinner? What shall I cook?"

Hannah shook her head and with a weary voice said, "Whatever you can find in the kitchen. Just cook whatever you can. I think Noah will be grateful for anything." Hannah continued walking up the stairs.

As soon as Hannah disappeared, her two small dogs ran into the room, both playing tug o' war with a small tree branch. "Get out, you two." The dogs ignored her. Rebecca placed Mason in the playpen with Rose. Now the two *bopplin* were crying together, which made them cry even louder. It was as if they were in competition, each trying to cry louder than the other.

Rebecca grabbed Annie, the beagle, by the collar

and led her outside. The terrier, Sophie, quickly followed, abandoning the tree branch. Now with the two dogs outside, Rebecca clipped the lock on the dog door so they would not come back in. Two naughty, young dogs and two crying *bopplin* were a little more than she could handle all at the one time.

Now, all she had to do was to calm the *bopplin* and cook the dinner at the same time. Rebecca shrugged and hoped that she would do a *gut* job of looking after everything while Hannah had a sleep. At least it would be *gut* experience for when she had *kinner* of her own. She found the pram in the utility room and sat the two *bopplin* in the pram and wheeled them up and down, hoping the motion would calm them while she looked for something to cook for dinner.

It worked; the twins remained quiet so long as Rebecca pushed them back and forth. With one hand on the handle of the pram, Rebecca gingerly made her way to the icebox where she found a leg of lamb and a chicken. There was no time to roast a leg of lamb so she pulled the chicken out and set it on the kitchen bench while wondering what to make out of it. There were plenty of vegetables in the box under the sink. Rebecca decided to make their *grossmammi's* chicken casserole. She knew the recipe well.

When Rebecca stopped pushing the pram, the twins immediately burst into loud wails. Rebecca needed two hands to prepare the meal, but finally found that if she sang at full volume, the *bopplin* stopped crying. She sang *Blessed Redeemer* loudly and hoped that no one would be able to hear her sing. Hopefully Hannah was not expecting any visitors. Rebecca nearly laughed every time she looked at Mason and Rose's faces, looking at her with wide eyes.

As she sang and pulled the chicken apart, she thought of Elijah and what their *kinner* would look like if they married. Surely they would look similar to Hannah and Noah's twins since they would be cousins. How nice it would be to have *bopplin* soon so they could grow up with Hannah and Noah's *kinner* and Esther and Jacob's *dochder*, Isabel.

Rebecca silently rebuked herself and pushed such silly thoughts from her mind. She could hardly marry Elijah just to have their *kinner* grow up with her *schweschders' kinner.*

The twins launched into a fresh bout of sniffling and looked as though they were about to cry again. Rebecca abandoned the chicken and hurried to push them once more. Finally the two fell asleep, leaning against each other. They looked so cute, that Rebecca felt tears sting her eyes. How beautiful they were. She admired them for a moment before she hurried to get the meal finished before they woke up and before Noah came home.

The next morning Rebecca awoke before dawn. She had been tossing and turning all night. Seeing Hannah's *bopplin* had made her heart yearn for *bopplin* of her own, yet how could she ever have any, when Elijah was the only *mann* she had ever loved and would ever love? She knew that. So then, what could she do? She didn't want to be all alone and living in a *grossmammi haus* behind one of her *schweschders'* houses. On the other hand, she couldn't enter a loveless marriage with someone. Should she marry Elijah even though he didn't love her?

Rebecca sat up in bed and rubbed her eyes hard. Today she and Mary were going to visit the widow, Mrs. Ramseyer, and clean her house. She stretched and then went downstairs to make *kaffi* in the predawn dark.

Mary was next into the kitchen, rubbing her eyes. "I didn't sleep well," she announced to Rebecca. "You look like you didn't sleep well either."

"No, I didn't," Rebecca admitted.

"Why? Was there something on your mind?"

Rebecca nodded. "Probably the same thing that's on your mind."

"*Menner!*" Mary said in disgust. "Oh well, helping Mrs. Ramseyer today should take our minds off it. The Flickingers won't mind you being away for the morning?"

"*Nee,*" Rebecca said. "Benjamin is their only guest at the moment and they are quite concerned for Mrs. Ramseyer. I think they feel a connection to her because of the horse, for some strange reason."

"Maybe the situation with the horse made everyone a little more aware of how much help she needs, perhaps," Mary said.

Soon, Mr. and Mrs. Miller came into the room. They all sat down and shared a large breakfast of bacon and eggs, fried potato, thick slices of homemade bread slathered with butter, as well as apple pie and maple syrup.

"Sarah and I will be running some errands in town today," Mrs. Miller said between mouthfuls of apple pie. "Rebecca and Mary, the two of you will be okay to help Mrs. Ramseyer?"

The two girls said that they would.

When Rebecca and Mary arrived at Mrs. Ramseyer's house, they took their horse to the barn, unhitched him, and put him into a stall with some hay. They walked around the front of the house, laden under the weight of sugar cream pies for Mrs. Ramseyer. She was sitting on a Sap Cherry rocking chair on the porch, waving to them. Rebecca thought she looked quite frail and was sorry Mrs. Ramseyer didn't have any *kinner* to look after her.

"*Hiya*, Rebecca and Mary," Mrs. Ramseyer said.

"*Mamm* sent these," Rebecca said by way of greeting. "We'll put them in the kitchen?"

"*Denki*," Mrs. Ramseyer said. "Would you mind going through? You know where the kitchen is."

Rebecca and Mary returned to the porch. "We'll get to work immediately," Rebecca said. "We'll start with cleaning the house, unless there something you would rather us do first?"

"*Nee, denki*," Mrs. Ramseyer said. "There's a lovely young *mann* coming over later to split the firewood for me."

Rebecca and Mary set about cleaning the house.

"There's an electric vacuum cleaner at the B&B," Rebecca told Mary in low tones as they were both sweeping.

"Yes, it would be good if there was a gas-powered broom," Mary said, and the two girls collapsed in helpless peals of laughter.

Rebecca was so used to working hard, she didn't

notice the time slipping away. Mrs. Ramseyer came inside and sank into the couch. "You girls will get too thin working so hard. I need to fatten you up. I'll make some lunch."

"Oh, we can make the lunch. *Mamm* sent some," Rebecca protested, but her words were drowned by someone knocking on the door.

"Who could that be?" Mrs. Ramseyer muttered. She got off the couch gingerly and made her way slowly to the door. She opened the door to reveal a happy Fannie Graber, the bishop's wife.

"I heard Rebecca and Mary were working hard here so I brought us all some lunch," Fannie said.

Rebecca and Mary exchanged glances, and Mrs. Ramseyer cleared her throat. "I'm not very hungry today," she said.

"Nonsense!" Mrs. Graber said. "You'll feel much better after you eat some of my food."

When everyone was seated around the dining table, Mrs. Fannie turned to Rebecca and Mary. "Why don't you set the table and I'll see to the lunch."

Mrs. Fannie Graber set a large pot on the table. Rebecca scarcely dared ask what was in it. *Maybe if I don't know what it is, it won't taste so bad*, she said silently to herself.

Mary, never one to hold back, asked, "What's in it, Mrs. Graber?"

"Why it's *schnitz un knepp*," she said.

Rebecca thought that a little plain and normal, and was puzzled as well as relieved. Rebecca loved the combination of ham, apples, and dumplings.

To her dismay, Fannie continued. "It's not the traditional recipe that was passed down to me by my grandmother. No, indeed. I've added sardines and chopped liver. I find those additions work well with just about anything."

Mrs. Ramseyer looked decidedly miserable for the first time that day. "I think I might just have lemonade. My stomach is unsettled, you see." Her eye twitched when she said it, and Rebecca thought Mrs. Ramseyer was probably feeling guilty for lying.

"I have just the drink to settle your stomach!" Fannie Graber exclaimed. "It is good for settling the stomach. It's a combination of tincture of peppermint, ginger juice, garlic, and fish oil. It is very high in Omega 3." As she poured some into a glass for the reluctant Mrs. Ramseyer, some spilled onto the table.

Rebecca looked at it, and considered it looked to be pure oil. She pulled an expression of distaste. Mrs. Graber insisted everyone eat up big, so Rebecca pretended to eat. She realized she wouldn't get away pretending for too long, because it would be plain to Fannie Graber that her plate would remain as full as ever.

She wished Mrs. Ramseyer had a pet dog or cat so she could slip the food under the table, but considered the food would probably be dangerous for animals to eat. If only they were eating in the garden, and then she could have tipped the food onto a plant.

Finally, there was nothing else for it. Rebecca had to eat. She held her breath and tried to eat at the same time. She soon found that was quite a difficult feat to accomplish. She had been told as a child that if someone pinches their nose, then they cannot taste food. She could hardly pinch her nose in front of everyone, but she thought holding her breath would have the same effect.

Mary followed suit. Both ate slowly. The fact that did not go unnoticed by Fannie Graber. "Why are you two girls eating so slowly?" she asked them. "Don't you have much of an appetite?"

Both girls assured her that they didn't, in fact, have much of an appetite. *And I'm not lying this time*, Rebecca thought. *I certainly don't have much of an appetite after seeing this food.* She felt awfully bad, because Fannie Graber had the kindest heart and would be dreadfully upset if she knew people did not like her food.

Soon, Mrs. Graber stood up. "Please don't mind if I don't help you clear the table, but I must get home to prepare lunch for my husband."

Rebecca thought the other two women looked awfully relieved. She opened the door for Mrs. Graber and watched her drive away.

"Now let's eat some food that won't make us sick," Mrs. Ramseyer said with a chuckle. "It's most kind of Fannie Graber to bring this food, but not everyone shares her exotic taste. I for one don't, and the garlic in that food makes me quite sick. Let's have some normal food to wash down the taste of the other. Why don't you see what you can find for lunch?" She addressed her questions to both the girls.

Mrs. Miller had actually sent along lunch, a huge baked ham salad with bologna and cheese spread sandwiches on thick slices of homemade bread, and Rebecca and Mary set it on the table. Just then there was another knock at the door. Rebecca held her breath, wondering if Mrs. Graber had returned. Surely Mrs. Graber would be offended when she saw food other than hers on the table.

Mrs. Ramseyer went to the door and opened it. "It's you," she exclaimed with obvious delight.

She stepped aside, and Rebecca and Mary saw Nash.

He narrowed his eyes. "What are you two doing here?" he asked them.

"We're helping Mrs. Ramseyer by cleaning her house and getting lunch," Mary said. "What are *you* doing here?"

"I'm seeing to the firewood," he said. "Rhoda is low with her supply."

Rebecca thought that awfully strange. She wondered what Nash was up to. Maybe he wasn't up to anything? Maybe he did have a kind heart under that rather strange and prickly exterior.

While she was still pondering this, Mrs. Ramseyer invited him on. "You've come at a *gut* time. We were about to have lunch. Come, join us. You need to have something to eat. You're way too thin as it is."

Nash thanked her politely and walked over to the table, his eyes alight. Once more, Rebecca figured that Nash must have gone without much food for a considerable period of time.

Nash took an empty bowl and filled it with Fannie Graber's version of *schnitz un knepp.* Before anyone could stop him, he greedily spooned some into his mouth.

"Mrs. Graber made that," Rebecca said, wondering how to word it so Nash would be warned, but she would still sound polite. "It has anchovies and chopped liver in it."

"Weird," Nash said. "It's good though."

Rebecca watched as Nash refilled his bowl several times.

After lunch, the girls intended to do some baking for Mrs. Ramseyer now that all the cleaning had been done. Nash stood up. "Do you need any fences fixed or anything?" he asked her.

She shook her head. "*Nee.* I don't think so, but would you mind checking them for me?"

"Sure. And how's the horse going?"

"*Wunderbar,*" Mrs. Ramseyer said.

Nash left the house. She turned to Rebecca and Mary. "What a wonderful young *mann*," she said. "He's been such a help to me. I don't know what I would have done if it wasn't for him."

"Nash?" Rebecca asked. She was somewhat confused.

"Just goes to show, doesn't it," Mary whispered to Rebecca. "*Gott* really does work in mysterious ways."

Chapter Twenty-One

"How long have those raisins been soaking now, Sarah?"

Sarah looked up at Rebecca. "It would be three hours by now. Will we make the funeral pies now?"

Rebecca nodded. "*Jah*, we'd better hurry or we'll be late. Good thing funeral pies keep well; there would be no time to make them tomorrow."

"Is Mrs. Flickinger doing all right?" Sarah's face was full of concern.

Rebecca tucked a stray strand of hair back under her *kapp*. "She is happy that her *mudder* is with *Gott* and has no more suffering, but she'll miss her, of course."

"And are you okay, Rebecca? I know you and *Grossmammi* Deborah were close."

"*Jah, denki,* Sarah. It's hard, but I know she's better off with *Gott*, there's no more pain or suffering."

Sarah simply nodded and beat a bowl of eggs. "It doesn't make it any easier at all for someone when they know that a friend or relative's time is nearly up and that they could go to be with *Gott* at any time, but I suppose at least it wasn't a shock."

Rebecca sighed and poured flour and sugar to a large mixing bowl. "Suppose."

"I feel sorry for Nash, though," Sarah said as she mixed the eggs with flour and sugar.

"Nash?"

"*Grossmammi* Deborah was Nash's *grossmammi*. I think everyone's misjudged Nash. I got into trouble when I was on *rumspringa*, and it's not if he's been baptized or anything. People judge him by the way he looks, and that's really not fair."

Rebecca decided it was best not to give her opinion; after all, Sarah's mind seemed made up. Rebecca did not trust Nash, not one little bit. She always did her best to avoid him, but there would be no avoiding him today. *Grossmammi* Deborah had passed away the day before, and today everyone would go to the B&B for the viewing. Tomorrow would be the funeral.

Rebecca stirred the eggs, sugar, flour, lemon juice, lemon rind, cornstarch, cinnamon, allspice, and water over the stove for fifteen minutes, while Sarah finished making the pastry. Finally the pies were made, covered with slender lengths of dough in a crisscrossed pattern, and now had to be baked until browned.

"These will only take around twenty-five minutes to go golden brown," Sarah said aloud to herself.

"Are you okay, Sarah?"

Sarah looked up from placing the pies in the oven. "*Jah*, why wouldn't I be?"

"You're talking to yourself."

Sarah's hand flew to her mouth.

Rebecca chuckled. "You only do that when you're stressed, I've noticed." Sarah just smiled politely and ducked her head, so Rebecca decided not to pursue the matter.

On the buggy ride to the B&B, which was only a short distance, Rebecca noticed that Sarah grew more and more anxious. She wrung her apron between her hands.

When Mr. Miller drew the *familye* buggy up to the B&B, the first person Rebecca saw was Nash. He, like everyone else on this occasion, was wearing black, but in his case, they were not Amish clothes. Still, he seemed more toned down than usual, and even from that distance, Rebecca could see that he had taken out all his piercings. She was glad that he had chosen to be respectful.

The Hostetler *familye* buggy, Noah and Hannah's buggy, and Moses and Martha's buggy all arrived at the same time as the Millers', and pulled in behind them. They all walked in together. Rebecca's heart leaped when she saw Elijah, and he gave her a warm smile.

There were no guests at the B&B, apart from Benjamin Shetler, who was more or less a permanent resident, so there were no *Englischers* to interrupt the solemn proceedings. To Rebecca's discomfort, Elijah accompanied Sarah into the reception rooms at the B&B.

The Miller and Hostetler *familyes* filed into the main living room, and greeted Mrs. Flickinger, who was doing her best not to cry. Mr. Flickinger stood close by her side. Many other members of the community were already there, all dressed in black and sitting around.

Mr. Flickinger asked the Miller and Hostetler *familyes* if they would like to see the body. They all politely said they would, then lined up in single file. Mrs. Hostetler stayed back to comfort Mrs. Flickinger while Mr. Flickinger took them to the plain, six-sided, pine coffin, the upper half of which was opened. He pulled back a white cloth to reveal *Grossmammi* Deborah's face.

Rebecca did not want to look at *Grossmammi* Deborah's face, although she knew that *Grossmammi* Deborah was no longer there and that her earthly body was just a garment. *Grossmammi* Deborah was in her wedding dress, and her face showed she was at peace. After briefly viewing *Grossmammi* Deborah, Rebecca slipped away to the kitchen, hoping no one had noticed her.

Rebecca stood at the kitchen window looking out over the snow drifting over the fields. *It's going to be an early winter*, she thought, wiping a stray tear or two away from her eyes. A noise behind her made her turn around.

"Are you okay?" Elijah was smiling down at her, his face full of warmth and concern.

Rebecca nodded, not trusting herself to speak. She had become quite close to *Grossmammi* Deborah and had enjoyed her conversations with her. *Grossmammi* Deborah's passing had left a void in her world. Her older *schweschders*, Hannah, Esther, and Martha, were all now married, and she had no one left to talk to. Sure, there was Sarah and Mary, but she did not feel she could confide in them too closely, and her *mudder* was not someone she could talk to as a friend; rather, she was an elder to be respected. Rebecca at once felt terribly sorry for herself, and to her dismay, burst into tears.

The next thing Rebecca knew was that Elijah's strong arms were around her. She took in his manly scent of honey and oatmeal soap, tinged with the woodsy scents of the farm. Rebecca did not want Elijah to let her go, but at the same time, was afraid someone would come upon them and think something untoward was going on.

Finally Elijah released her and held her at arms' length. "Here, sit down, Rebecca. I'll make you some hot meadow tea. I'll put sugar in it. I know you were close to *Grossmammi* Deborah."

"*Denki*, Elijah." Rebecca sat down and sniffled. Her heart was racing from Elijah's proximity. Was he being considerate because he cared for her, or simply because he was a good, thoughtful person? She had no way of knowing. If only Elijah would give her some sign of his feelings toward her.

Elijah placed the tea down in front of Rebecca, and sat opposite her, smiling. "See, I keep telling you that I'd make a *gut* husband."

Rebecca could not help but laugh. "*Jah*, you would."

Elijah was on the point of saying something further, when Sarah burst into the kitchen. She too had been crying. Rebecca had no idea why, as Sarah had not known *Grossmammi* Deborah. Benjamin Shetler hurried into the kitchen right behind Sarah, and Sarah and Benjamin both stopped and stood there with their mouths open when they saw Elijah and Rebecca.

Elijah stood up. "Sarah, is anything the matter?"

Sarah hung her head, so Elijah guided her to a seat. "I've just made Rebecca some meadow tea, so I'll make you some too."

"*Denki.*" Sarah's voice was small and quiet.

Rebecca's heart fell. *So, Elijah was just being nice to me because he's a caring person*, she thought, *and now he's being exactly the same to Sarah too.* Rebecca felt like a third wheel, and Benjamin had already left. Without a word, she stood up and left the room.

Elijah was a little upset. He had been about to ask Rebecca to go on a buggy ride, when Sarah and Benjamin Shetler had hurried into the kitchen. Why had Rebecca hurried out, straight after Benjamin Shetler? He hoped Rebecca did not have feelings for Benjamin. After all, he was just as handsome as Nash, although in a different way. What other reason would Rebecca have for charging out of the kitchen like that? He had wanted to follow her, but Sarah was upset. *I need to speak to Rebecca as soon as possible*, he thought, with growing urgency.

Nash Grayson was upset that his grandmother had died. She had never been mean to him, not like his own mother and father had, but on the bright side, he figured that there was a very good chance she had left him something in her will. Perhaps it was enough to pay off his gambling debts. If not, it might be enough for him to bet on just one more race to make some good money.

Nash wondered how long it would be before the will

would be read, and then after that, how long it would take him to be paid any inheritance. Then he could escape from this dreadful, dreary place. He'd go mad if he had to stay with these people too much longer. All they cared about were other people and God; it was just not natural.

Nash couldn't believe his luck when he saw Rebecca, Elijah, Sarah, and Benjamin go into the kitchen, but only Benjamin and Rebecca come out. He sneaked to the door and leaned against it, straining his ears to hear what they were saying. To his great disappointment, Elijah appeared to be lecturing Sarah about God. All Elijah was doing was telling Sarah what the ministers had said.

Nash sighed, but then he had a thought. Rebecca herself had no idea what Elijah was doing in there with Sarah, and he could use this to his advantage. Nash smiled to himself as he headed to the closest plate of free food.

Chapter Twenty-Two

"It's just like one of those movies that my roommate, Sheryl Garner, made me watch when I was on *rumspringa*," Martha said. "What was the name of it again?" She was met with blank looks, so continued, "With the three of us *schweschders* being married, and now the funeral today—oh I know, the movie was called *Four Weddings and a Funeral*."

"Martha!" Mrs. Miller shrieked. "You apologize at once."

Martha appeared puzzled. "Who to? What for?"

Her *mudder* simply glared at her and hurried into the kitchen, banging pots and pans. Moses winked at Martha and she giggled guiltily.

Rebecca watched the whole exchange. *If only Elijah felt the same way about me that Moses clearly feels about Martha*, she thought, *and then it would be four weddings and not just three.*

Several minutes later, the *familye* climbed into their buggies to drive the short distance to the B&B for the funeral, Martha and Moses in one buggy, and Mr. and Mrs. Miller, Rebecca, Mary, and Sarah, in the other. The former cheerful mood turned more somber the closer they came to the B&B. In fact, Sarah was still in her subdued, quiet mood of the day before.

Upon arrival, Rebecca saw many people she didn't know, and figured they were from the Flickingers' former community. After all, the Flickingers had not been in town long at all.

When they arrived, Elijah walked over to Rebecca, Mary, and Sarah, and Rebecca noted, to her discomfort, that Sarah smiled at him widely. Elijah helped the women carry the food they had prepared into the B&B, but when they were halfway to the building, Nash hurried over to them. "Is there anything I can do to help?"

"*Denki*, Nash." Sarah smiled sweetly at him. "You could go and help Mrs. Miller bring in more food."

Nash hurried over to find Mrs. Miller, and the three continued on their way.

"He seems very nice and thoughtful," Sarah said, but Rebecca noted that Elijah looked displeased at her statement. Could he be jealous of Sarah's admiration for Nash?

The service started soon after everyone was inside the B&B. One of the ministers stood up and addressed everyone present. He said that death is the act of *Gelassenheit*, the final surrender to *Gott*. The minister then read the words of a hymn, for, like at all Amish funerals, hymns are read by the minister rather than sung.

Consider, O man!
Consider your death, the end.

Death often comes unawares.
He who is strong and glowing today,
Tomorrow or sooner, may.
Pass away.

Another minister then read prayers from the *Die Ernsthafte Christenpflicht*, "Prayer Book for Earnest Christians." Afterward, he spoke on the hope of the resurrection, and in English rather than in Pennsylvania Dutch. Rebecca looked around to see if there were any *Englisch* visitors, for, at funerals, ministers usually only spoke in the English language for the benefit of *Englischer* visitors. She could only see Nash. He saw her looking at him and smiled widely at her. Rebecca was then aware that Elijah was watching the two of them. *I hope he's jealous*, she thought, *as that might spur him into action*. Then her stomach churned. *He probably likes Sarah and not me*, she thought.

Around ninety minutes later, everyone returned to their buggies for the solemn procession to the cemetery. Mrs. Miller was standing by the *familye* buggy, her hands on her hips. "Hurry, Rebecca, find Sarah. I can't find her anywhere. Run along now."

Rebecca turned around and hurried back in the direction of the B&B.

"Looking for someone?" Nash was sitting on the front porch.

"Yes, Sarah. Have you seen her?"

Nash stood up and walked over to Rebecca. "Last I saw her, she was kissing Elijah," he said in a conspiratorial whisper.

Rebecca could not hide the horrified look on her face. "What?" she gasped.

"Oh, I'm not supposed to know," Nash said. "Just because I'm an *Englischer* now, I suppose I'm not meant to know all your secrets. I didn't find out deliberately. I saw you walk out of the kitchen yesterday, so I walked in, and Elijah and Sarah were kissing. I apologized and left as soon as I could. They sure looked guilty." Nash laughed unkindly.

Rebecca felt as if she would pass out. Her surroundings seemed to be receding. Just then, her *mudder's* shrill voice pierced her thoughts. "Rebecca! Rebecca! Hurry, Sarah's here."

Rebecca hurried back to the buggy and climbed aboard, shooting a look at Sarah. *Sarah sure looks guilty*, Rebecca thought. Rebecca did not trust Nash, but would he go so far as to tell an outright lie? He did know that Elijah and Sarah were alone in the kitchen so he might have based a story on that.

The Millers' buggy fell into procession behind the horse-drawn hearse containing the coffin, and the funeral party soon arrived at the cemetery. Rebecca felt as if it were all a dream, as if it were happening to someone else.

Some of the *menner* in the community had already dug the grave by hand. One of the ministers spoke briefly at the graveside stating that *Grossmammi* Deborah was no longer here but with *Gott*, and then the coffin was lowered while a minister read a hymn.

Rebecca felt dizzy and somewhat nauseous, and was unable to concentrate, and the fact that she felt guilty over this only made matters worse. *Have I truly lost Elijah?* she asked herself. *How could I have been so silly? Grossmammi Deborah and Aenti Irene were right, I should have married him and let his love for me come later.*

On the other hand, was it possible that Nash was lying? Yet what motive could he have for doing so? Still, that would explain why Sarah was so nervous about going to the viewing and to the funeral, because she didn't want Rebecca to see her with Elijah.

Rebecca put her hands to her head. All the thoughts running around in her head were bringing on a headache. Already there was a dull throbbing in her temples.

People were starting to leave the cemetery, to head back to the B&B for a meal, which had been prepared in advance by the women of the community.

Rebecca was still wrestling with her thoughts, when she saw Elijah over by some gravestones. At first she thought he might be reading the German names on the older gravestones, but then he approached Sarah. He handed her a small slip of paper. She opened it, and smiled widely up at Elijah. Rebecca fought back tears. Clearly it was a written invitation of sorts. The facts were clear: Rebecca had lost Elijah, and he was now dating Sarah.

Elijah had seen Nash speak to Rebecca on the porch, and had seen Rebecca's upset expression moments later. He did not trust Nash, but Sarah seemed to have a good opinion of him, which meant that Rebecca might too. *I'll bet Nash is up to no good*, Elijah thought.

To make matters worse, Elijah had walked off by himself, hoping Rebecca would seek him out. The two of them often had private conversations, but his every attempt to speak to Rebecca after he had decided to ask her to marry him had been thwarted. He had to give Sarah the note from his *mudder*, and his timing could not have been worse. He had looked up to see Rebecca watching them, and then she had turned away. Elijah sent up a silent petition to *Gott*. *Please Gott, help things come right for me. I am making a mess of things by myself.*

Chapter Twenty-Three

Rebecca was lying in the herb garden by the lavenders, feeling sorry for herself. She liked to lie on the ground. It helped her think. Rebecca cringed when she heard footsteps, as her mother always scolded her for lying in the dirt. When she saw it was Mary walking around aimlessly, she called out to her. "Mary, is something wrong?"

When Mary walked over, Rebecca was concerned to see Mary had been crying.

Mary sat on the ground next to Rebecca. "It's David Yoder," she said.

"What's he done?" Rebecca asked with concern.

"Nothing, that's the problem. He hasn't done anything. Rebecca, this is terrible. I've made up my mind."

"What are you going to do?" Rebecca tried to come up with some possibilities in her mind, but could not think of any.

"The next time I see David, I'm going to tell him that I like him."

"You are?" Rebecca thought that very brave of Mary.

"He might always tell me he doesn't like me back," Mary said, "but at least then I will know and I can move on with my life. It's been too long, and now I really need to know. The only thing is, I don't want it to change our friendship."

Rebecca nodded. She could not think of any wise words to offer.

Mary regarded her for some time before asking, "Do you think that's the right thing to do?"

Rebecca thought about it some more, and then said, "I don't know what to do. I wouldn't know what to do if I were you, but yes, I think I would ask him. Otherwise you'll never know."

"Actually, I'm afraid to do it, but I think I have to." Mary seemed to be talking to herself rather than to Rebecca. "I hope I have the courage to go through with it, though."

"Say to yourself that you will ask him the next time you see him, and when you do see him, blurt it out without thinking about it first. I think you need to talk yourself into it ahead of time. Otherwise you won't go through with it, and you'll be upset."

Mary rubbed her eyes with one hand. "Yes, I think you're right. That's what I'll do. The next time I see David, I'll tell him how I feel about him. Anyways, have you seen Sarah?"

Rebecca shook her head. "She's gone. She's taken the buggy and gone visiting."

Mary looked surprised. "Who is she visiting? She didn't tell me she was going. Is she visiting a boy?"

Rebecca gave half a nod and then shook her head. "Perhaps she's running errands for *Mamm*, or she could be visiting Elijah."

"Why would she visit Elijah?"

Before Rebecca could reply, they heard the clip clop of a horse's hooves. "Maybe that's her now," Mary said, standing up. She ducked back down with her hand over her mouth. "Oh no! It's David Yoder. I'm going to have to tell him, aren't I?"

Rebecca nodded. "I'm afraid so. Otherwise you'll be annoyed with yourself."

"What's he doing here?" Mary said. When the sound of the buggy got closer, Mary stood up. "*Hiya*, David."

He settled his horse, which had given a little shy at Mary suddenly standing up. "Mary, my *mudder* sent me with these banana cream pies for Mrs. Miller."

"David, I have something important to tell you."

Rebecca was embarrassed, lying there behind the cover of lavenders. Should she stand up now? If she did, she would no doubt break Mary's confidence, but if she stayed, then it would be even worse when she was discovered. She didn't know what to do so didn't move a muscle. From her position on the ground, she could see Mary wringing her hands nervously.

"What is it?" David said.

"I like you."

David laughed. "I like you too."

"No, I don't mean I like you," Mary said.

"You don't like me?" Rebecca thought David sounded hurt.

"Yes, I do like you, of course. Of course, I like you.

When I said I liked you, I meant I liked you, but it also meant I *liked* you. Don't you realize what I'm trying to say?"

There was silence, so Rebecca assumed David was shaking his head. Mary pushed on. "David, you're being quite thick. Don't you understand what I'm trying to say? I really like you, I said. I have feelings for you."

Mary heard David gasp and then she heard noises that sounded like he was getting out of the buggy. Soon she heard footsteps walking over to Mary. "You have feelings for me, Mary?"

He sounds awfully surprised, Rebecca thought. Her heart skipped a beat. *Did he sound pleased, or was that just my imagination?*

"Yes, and I have had for ages. Now you need to tell me if you have feelings for me. If you don't, that's fine. We can be friends and keep sharing Pirate. That's fine. I mean it, David. I don't want anything to get awkward between us. And things won't get awkward between us if you don't have feelings for me."

"But, but..." David sputtered.

"What do you have to say for yourself?" Rebecca saw Mary put her hands on her hips. She felt awful being party to such a conversation, but she could hardly stand up now and break the moment. She held her breath, hoping dearly that David would tell Mary he had feelings for her.

"Is this a joke, Mary?" David asked her.

Mary sighed long and hard. "*Nee*, it is not a joke. I've had feelings for you for a long time."

"I never knew that."

"Well, you do now." Mary's voice held more than a hint of annoyance. "Just tell me whether you have feelings for me or not!"

Rebecca had her eyes shut tightly, almost willing David to say he had feelings for Mary, but there was a long silence. *Poor Mary,* she thought. *David hasn't said a word.* Rebecca opened her eyes and was shocked to see David and Mary kissing.

At that point David saw Rebecca lying in the herb garden and stopped kissing Mary at once.

Rebecca struggled to her feet. "Please forgive me," she said, dusting down her apron. "I was lying in the herb garden with my thoughts. When Mary came over, we chatted. I didn't mean to eavesdrop."

David's mouth was still hanging open. Clearly, he had been rendered speechless. Rebecca walked into the house, taking big strides. When she was inside, she peeked out the window.

"What are you peeking out the window for?" Mrs. Miller's loud voice boomed behind her.

Rebecca didn't know what to say. "It's David and Mary," she said.

Her mother pushed past her and looked out the window. "Oh! Oh!" she said.

"What's happening?" Rebecca asked her.

"It's not good to eavesdrop, Rebecca," Mrs. Miller snapped.

"But we can't hear them from here," Rebecca said. Sometimes her mother could be awfully unreasonable. "They were kissing before."

"You must not repeat such information, Rebecca,"

her mother scolded her and then looked out the curtains once more.

When she turned around, she was smiling. "Rebecca, quick, fetch some sugar cakes and some Shoo-fly pie for our guest."

Rebecca walked into the kitchen. She cut the Shoo-fly pie into sections and put the pieces on plates. She went out into the living room and saw her mother still peeping around the curtains.

"Rebecca, have you prepared the food for our guest?"

"*Jah, Mamm*," Rebecca said.

"*Gut*." Her mother sat on a couch and picked up some knitting. Moments later, there was a knock on the door. "Who could that be?" Mrs. Miller called out in a loud voice. "Rebecca, would you get that?"

Rebecca showed in David and Mary. Both their faces were beet red. Rebecca assumed Mary's was from happiness and David's was from both embarrassment and happiness. Rebecca too was embarrassed at overhearing the conversation.

Mrs. Miller looked up. "David! What a lovely surprise. Come in, we were about to eat."

"My mother sent me with these banana cream pies for you," David said, handing them to Mrs. Miller.

"Please tell her I said thank you. Here, Rebecca take this to the kitchen."

When Rebecca returned, David and Mary were sitting next to each other on the couch, and Mrs. Miller was beaming at them.

"So then, David, will you be taking Mary on a buggy ride soon?"

"How did you know?" he asked.

"I know a lot of things," Mrs. Miller said smugly. "And you haven't answered my question, young man."

David appeared flustered. "Yes, yes I am. I'm taking Mary on a buggy ride right now. That is, with your permission, Mrs. Miller."

"Of course you have my permission." Mrs. Miller beamed at him.

David and Mary ate pie and drank some meadow tea faster than Rebecca had ever seen anyone eat or drink, and then left.

At least it's turning out happily for some, Rebecca thought. *I will end up here all alone, like Aenti Irene* said. *Mary will marry David, and Sarah will marry Elijah, and I'll be here with Mamm.* Tears pricked at her eyes, and she wiped them away surreptitiously, hoping her mother wouldn't notice.

Later that day Mrs. Miller was reading and Rebecca was making noodles, when she heard Mary return. She hurried outside. "Where are you going?" Mrs. Miller said.

"To fetch more peppermint," Rebecca said.

As soon Rebecca was outside, she saw David Yoder was already driving away. Mary had not yet reached the first porch step. Rebecca was relieved she had not happened upon another private moment.

She grabbed Mary by the hand and took her into the vegetable garden. She picked some peppermint in case she forgot, and her mother remarked on the fact. "Tell me everything!" she said to Mary.

Mary could scarcely contain her excitement. "David and I are getting married."

Rebecca could scarcely believe her ears. "*Wunderbar!*"

Mary nodded. "I can't believe it. He's been in love with me for years, just like I've been in love with him for years! He was certain I only thought of him as a friend just like I thought he only thought of me as a friend."

"Did he tell you why he never asked you on buggy ride?" Rebecca asked her.

Mary nodded. "His *schweschder*, Jessie, told him I was dating a *mann* back in my community and was promised to him, but was staying here until Mrs. Miller didn't need my help anymore."

"That Jessie Yoder!" Rebecca said crossly.

"And you know all the times I've gone home to see my parents and my brother?"

Rebecca nodded.

"Jessie told David I had been seeing this imaginary *mann*."

Rebecca scratched her head. "But surely he knows his own *schweschder* well enough to know she tells terrible lies."

Mary held up both hands, palms upward. "Obviously not! He did say he had been plucking up the courage to ask me about the *mann*."

"It's strange he never got around to asking you about this imaginary person."

"He said he wanted to, but he said he'd be too upset to hear about him," Mary said. "Can you believe it,

Rebecca? David Yoder has been in love with me all this time?"

"It's wonderful news," Rebecca said. "I'm so happy for the two of you."

"He hasn't even met my parents yet," Mary continued. "He's going to pay a driver to take him to my parents and he's going to ask my father's permission to marry me."

Rebecca clasped hands. "I'm so happy for you!" she exclaimed.

"Look, here's Sarah! She'll be shocked!"

Rebecca followed Mary's gaze and saw Sarah driving a buggy in her direction. Her spirits fell. Had Sarah been to visit Elijah?

It was obvious now. Her previous fears were now confirmed, after all. Mary was going to marry David, and Sarah was going to marry Elijah, her Elijah. Where had it all gone so wrong?

Chapter Twenty-Four

"Wherever have you been, Sarah?" Mary asked her.

Two bright red dots broke out on Sarah's cheeks. "I had to visit someone about someone."

"Was it something to do with a boy?" the ever-forthright Mary asked her.

Sarah put her hands over her face and then at once led the horse toward the barn.

So, I was right, Rebecca thought. *Sarah has been speaking to Elijah and she doesn't want to tell me, because she knows it would hurt my feelings.* She felt as though she had been stabbed through the heart.

Rebecca frantically brushed away the tears that fell unbidden. She hurried into the house, passing her mother on the way. Mrs. Miller called out, but Rebecca ignored her. As Rebecca had been barefoot, she put on her sturdy shoes and then walked back to the front of the house.

"Where are you going, Rebecca?" her mother called after her.

"I need to be by myself to think and pray," she said.

Mrs. Miller hesitated, and Rebecca held her breath, thinking her mother would ask her to help in the kitchen. However, Mrs. Miller did not. "Off you go. But don't be away long. There's a storm coming in and it's going to be a cold night. This is going to be an early winter."

Rebecca walked back out into the chill of the late afternoon air, going down by the barn and taking a shortcut across the fields to the pond. She wandered aimlessly alongside the pond first. "I'll go back when I feel a little better," Rebecca said aloud to herself and kept walking.

Usually, Rebecca was comforted by the sight of birds such as the Northern Cardinals, the Gray Catbirds, and the Ruffled Grouse, by the wildflowers in colors of crimson, orange, and pink, and by the rippling water on the pond itself, but today there was no solace to be found.

Rebecca wiped her tears on her apron and kept marching on.

She was lost with her thoughts. It must be true. Where else could Sarah have been? Sarah had never shown any interest in any young man in the community. Yes, it had to be Elijah. Rebecca kept clutching at straws trying to discover how it must be someone else, but she couldn't come up with a logical reason. She kept crying and stumbling forward.

Before long, Rebecca realized that the sun was disappearing behind the horizon. She looked around and saw unfamiliar territory.

Where was she? Rebecca had never walked this far before. She now had lost all sense of direction as she had wandered away from the pond. She craned her neck to look for houses, but none were in plain sight, only the rolling hills and the poplars, beech, and birch trees.

Rebecca remembered when Martha had looked for Sam when he had gotten lost in the woods, and she remembered Martha discussing it later with Gary and Laura. Gary had said at the time that if someone is lost, they should not try to find their way out. They should simply stay where they are and wait for help to come to them.

Surely I'm not lost? Rebecca thought and then looked around her once more. What if she did try to find her way home and ended up walking in the other direction? She had no idea where north was or in which direction to walk to reach her house.

Finally, overcome by feeling sorry for herself, Rebecca sank under a falling log and sobbed, clutching her woollen cloak around her.

It was now almost dark and Rebecca was awfully cold. What's more, it was raining. Although the rain was light, a storm was coming in and Rebecca knew it would soon rain much more heavily. Where could she shelter? She couldn't see anywhere that would afford her protection from the rain and the cold.

"How far am I from my house?" Rebecca wondered. She tried to think how long she had been walking. She finally figured she must be several miles away, but in which direction?

Mr. Miller called the Hostetler barn from his workshop. As it happened, Elijah was the one to answer.

He was stricken by what Mr. Miller had said. Rebecca was missing. She had gone out for a walk and had not returned.

Elijah felt as though his heart stopped beating for a moment. He ran into the house to tell his mother. "*Mamm*, Rebecca Miller is missing."

Her mother looked up shocked, a soup ladle in her hand. "Missing? What do you mean?"

"She went for a walk and didn't return," Elijah explained. "Mr. Miller just called the barn."

Katie Hostetler made a shooing motion with her hand. "Off you go. Help the *menner* search."

Elijah didn't need to be told twice. He harnessed up his horse, for once grateful his horse was fast, and headed at a fast trot to the Millers' house.

"Has she come home yet?" he asked Mrs. Miller.

"*Nee*." Mrs. Miller was wringing her hands in obvious distress. "My husband has gone looking for her along the pond."

Elijah's heart caught in his mouth. He realized Mr. Miller was concerned maybe Rebecca had fallen in the pond and drowned. He forced himself to start breathing again.

"Pirate could find her," Mary said. "David and I have been training Pirate to track and he's quite good at it. I just need to take something of Rebecca's."

"I'm sure it won't work, but it's worth a try," Mrs. Miller said. "Mary, hurry and fetch something of Rebecca's. Elijah, could you take Mary to the Yoders' to fetch the dog?"

Soon, although not soon enough for Elijah, he was

driving Mary to the Yoders' house. Mary was clutching one of Rebecca's aprons to her. David Yoder met them at the front of the house. "We're all setting off to search now," he said. "*Mamm* has gone to tell some other *familyes* and my vadder has gone to fetch the bishop."

"I'm going to take Pirate," Mary told David. "He can he can track her."

David tapped himself in the side of the head. "Why didn't I think of that? That's a good idea, Mary. Do you think it will work?"

Mary shrugged. "It can't hurt."

David fetched Pirate's leash and handed the dog to Mary. "Are you going with Elijah?"

Mary looked at Elijah. He had often thought there was something between Mary and David, and he wondered why nothing had ever come of it. Still, now was not the time worried about such matters. "Hurry up Mary," he called out.

Mary gave it a little shrug and hurried over to the buggy with Pirate. "Will I give Pirate the scent now?" she asked Elijah.

Elijah was so muddleheaded with worry, he could scarcely think straight. He had to force his thoughts into order for a moment, and then he said, "*Nee*. Let's go back to the Millers' *haus* and then try to track her from there. We'll need to go on foot."

All the way back to the Millers' *haus*, Elijah was hoping Rebecca would have been found by the time they got there. He sent up a silent prayer to *Gott* to keep her safe and to have her found with the utmost haste.

Elijah could tell from a distance that no one had

found Rebecca as he approached the house. "We'll have to go on foot," he told Mr. Miller, who had returned and was about to search another direction.

"Rachel told me you're going to try to have the dog track her," he said.

Mrs. Miller hurried out with a flask and a thick coat and handed them to Elijah. "Here, she will need this hot *kaffi* when you find her. She will be cold and will need this coat."

"I'll go too," Sarah said. "I can't sit around here doing nothing and only the *menner* are out searching. I can carry the coat and the thermos."

"Are we ready?" Mary asked. Without waiting for a response, she put Rebecca's apron under Pirate's nose and said some words to him. Elijah couldn't hear what she said as his stomach was twisted into knots. He was sick to the stomach with worry.

Pirate took off at a good pace and Elijah's spirits lifted. Maybe the dog was able to track Rebecca, after all. Pirate headed across the fields and came to the pond, which made Elijah hold his breath. What if Rebecca had fallen in? He shook his head. No, he couldn't think like that. Surely she was all right. *Gott* had appointed one woman for every man and one man for every woman, and *Gott* would not let his beloved Rebecca fall into a pond.

Pirate hesitated by the pond and then followed it along for a little ways before heading away from the pond. Elijah breathed a long sigh of relief.

It was raining heavily by now, and the rain turned to sleet. Little bits of sleet stung Elijah's face, but all he could think about was Rebecca. Where was she? She was out in the dark, all alone in the sleet and the rain.

"Do you think this is working?" Sarah asked Mary, "or is Pirate just wandering off doing his own thing?"

"Well, we've never had him on a training exercise like this before," Mary said, "but he was getting awfully good at it besides."

Elijah agreed. "The dog certainly seems to have a sense of purpose," he said. "It's clear he doesn't think he is just out for a walk." He heard a shriek, and Sarah flew past him, falling hard.

Sarah picked herself up and dusted herself off. "Of all the places to fall, I would have to fall into a huge puddle," she said.

"You're going to be cold, Sarah," Elijah said, "as you're soaking wet now. Maybe you should have some of that hot *kaffi* now."

"I will when we find Rebecca," she said.

Pirate walked farther into the darkness. Elijah was relieved that the moon was still shining through the clouds and they could see where they were going. He then began to worry that perhaps Rebecca had fallen in a hole and hurt herself. He wondered if he should call out her name, but then figured he should wait until Pirate stopped looking.

That thought made him stricken with grief. What if Pirate *did* stop looking? What then? What would Elijah do? Elijah shook his head as if to dispel the thoughts. Soon, Pirate pulled away from Mary and ran. Mary fell forward onto the ground. Sarah and Elijah stopped to help her up. "Are you all right?" Sarah asked her.

"I think he's going to Rebecca," Mary said excitedly, and took off in the direction of the dog.

Elijah ran after her. "Don't run, Mary. It's not safe in the dark," he said.

Just then, he heard a voice call out, "Is anyone there?"

Elijah sprinted off in the direction of the voice, not caring whether or not it was safe. He saw the dog standing there, but then he realized Pirate was standing over Rebecca, who was sitting in the dubious shelter of a fallen log.

"Elijah," she said, and she burst into tears.

Elijah called over his shoulder. "Hurry! She's here. Sarah, hurry."

Sarah ran forward and Elijah helped Rebecca to her feet. "Are you all right? Are you hurt? What happened?" His words tumbled out one after the other.

Rebecca's teeth were chattering so much she could hardly speak. "I'm not hurt. I'm very cold," she said. "I was just walking, and I got lost and I thought I should wait to be found rather than get lost anymore." At least that's what Elijah thought she said because her teeth were chattering so much that it made her speech hard to understand.

He took the coat from Sarah and wrapped it around Rebecca tightly. "Quick Mary, give Rebecca some *kaffi,*" he said. Elijah watched Rebecca as she sipped the coffee tentatively. "Drink up," he encouraged her. "It will warm you up. Can you walk? Are you sure you're not hurt?"

"I can walk," she said.

Elijah took off his coat and gave it to Sarah, who was

shivering after her earlier fall into the puddle. "Are you all right, Sarah?" he asked her.

She staggered, so Elijah put one hand over her elbow.

Elijah knew where they were, as he had played in these parts many a time when young, with his *bruders*. Still, it was hard to see in the dark, and he had to make his way slowly with Rebecca on one arm and Sarah on the other. Both were shivering and their teeth were chattering. Mary kept patting Pirate and telling him what a good dog he was.

"He *is* a good dog," Elijah said. "A very good dog. I'm going to have to get him a very big treat for this."

Rebecca was so relieved when she saw Pirate that she burst into a fresh bout of tears. What a clever dog he was. She put her arms around his neck and tried to sob into his neck, but Pirate had other ideas. He slurped all over her face. This time, she didn't mind.

Rebecca looked up into Elijah's face. In the scant moonlight, she thought his face was edged with worry. He pulled her to her feet and asked her if she was all right, but then he soon asked Sarah if she was all right and he gave Sarah his coat.

Wasn't Rebecca the one who had been missing, not Sarah? Rebecca's spirits fell. If she wanted cold hard proof, now she had it. Elijah was clearly in love with Sarah. Tears fell flowed freely down her cheeks, but she didn't care. It was dark and there was no one to see them.

Chapter Twenty-Five

It was slow going. Rebecca leaned heavily on Elijah, but she didn't want him to think she was being forward. After all, she now knew about Elijah and Sarah, but it was obviously a secret, so she couldn't let on that she knew. Her heart was breaking.

It's all my fault for not letting him know how I felt about him sooner, she thought. Still, since Elijah wasn't in love with her, then her own feelings were hardly relevant. Every now and then Mary stopped to give Rebecca and Sarah some hot *kaffi*. Elijah was being attentive to both of them. *He is so kind hearted*, Rebecca thought. *And I feel sorry for Sarah getting hurt while looking for me. It was my own silly fault I got hurt.*

Rebecca thought she must apologize to Sarah as soon as she got the chance. But right now she was too tired and weary even to speak.

When they were close to the Millers' house, Elijah said to Mary, "Why don't you go ahead and tell the others that we found Rebecca, so they won't worry?"

Mary and Pirate ran off.

Soon, Mr. Miller and Noah Hostetler hurried to meet them. Rebecca managed to find her voice and tell them she was okay just very cold. "Sarah's cold too. She fell in a puddle and she's drenched and cold," Rebecca managed to say.

Mr. Miller took Rebecca's arm and helped her to the house, leaving Elijah alone with Sarah. Rebecca cast a wistful glance over her shoulder, only to see Elijah being awfully attentive to Sarah. She figured she would have to stop looking. It would only hurt, and maybe she would get over it in time. If only she had listened to the wise words of *Aenti* Irene.

Rebecca slowly walked to the house with Mr. Miller. Mrs. Miller was waiting on the front porch, holding a kerosene lamp. She looked awfully pleased to see Rebecca. "Where are the others? Where are Sarah and Elijah?" she asked Mr. Miller.

"They're not far behind me," Mr. Miller said. "Sarah fell into a puddle and she's cold and wet too." Mrs. Miller shook her head and clicked her tongue.

Mrs. Miller wasted no time organizing the girls to have a shower and then get into some warm clothes. Noah Hostetler went to the barn to call everyone to call people who had phones in their barns to put the word around, while Mr. Miller stoked the fire.

The warm water finally warmed Rebecca right through. It took a while for her to feel thoroughly warm, because she felt weirdly cold on the inside. She stood under the shower for a full five minutes until every part of her felt warm. Still, she did her best to hurry so

Sarah would not be delayed taking a shower. After her shower, she went downstairs and sat in front of the fire.

Elijah was still there. "How are you?" he asked her.

"*Gut*, *denki*," she responded automatically.

"And how is Sarah?" he asked her.

Rebecca's heart sank. She didn't think she could be any sadder than she was right at that moment. "She's fine too, *denki*. You'll see her in a minute."

She thought a momentary look of confusion passed over Elijah's face.

Mrs. Miller pressed a steaming mug of hot lemon tea into Rebecca's hands. "Drink this hot lemon tea with maple syrup."

Rebecca sipped the tea ever so slowly, but by the time she was halfway through, she was beginning to feel considerably better. Sarah came down the stairs and she too sat by the fire. Mrs. Miller put a blanket around her and fussed over her.

"Elijah, thank you so much for finding Rebecca, and thank you too, Mary."

Rebecca looked up and did a double take when she saw Pirate lying at Mary's feet, warming himself by the fire. Mrs. Miller had actually allowed the dog inside. Rebecca figured her mother must be awfully relieved to have her home, after all.

Rebecca clutched her blanket to her. She was nice and toasty warm near the fire, but all she wanted to do was sleep. She could not yet sleep, however, because Elijah was sitting opposite her, making her heart race.

"You will not be able to go to work tomorrow," Mrs. Miller said, but for once she did not speak in her usual scolding tone. "Never mind," she added, "I will drive to the Flickingers and explain the situation."

"I'm so glad you're all right," Elijah said, "and you too, Sarah."

Just then, Tom, Sarah's ginger cat jumped up to sit on Sarah's knee. At that point the cat noticed Pirate. The cat made the most horrible sound Rebecca had ever heard and lunged at Pirate. Pirate yelped and ran behind the couch.

Mrs. Miller laughed, as did Sarah and Mary. Elijah chuckled, but Rebecca thought she would never laugh again. Her heart was too broken. There was Elijah, sitting in the living room making polite conversation while her heart was breaking. All the while, he was hiding the fact that he and Sarah were dating.

The following morning, Rebecca awoke with a dreadful cold. Her mother took one look at her and told her to sit by the fire. "You're certainly not doing any work today," she said.

Sarah was fifteen minutes late to breakfast. Her face was swollen and her cheeks were red. "You're in no fit state for work either," Mrs. Miller said. "I insist you both stay inside all day and rest."

"How long did Elijah stay last night?" Rebecca asked Sarah when they were both sitting by the fire sipping hot meadow tea.

"I'm not sure," Sarah said.

Rebecca wondered if Sarah was being deliberately evasive, or whether she too had actually fallen asleep. She didn't want to press the issue in case Sarah became suspicious and thought she knew about the two of them.

Rebecca soon dozed off in the chair again. Her throat was raw and she had the beginnings of a headache. Mrs. Miller materialized beside her and dabbed peppermint oil on her forehead.

"*Nee, Mamm*, I don't like peppermint oil on my head."

"Nor do I, but I dislike headaches even more," her mother said in a self-satisfied voice. "Sarah, do you have a headache too?"

"*Nee, nee*," Sarah said hurriedly.

Rebecca wondered if Sarah did indeed have a headache but wasn't going to tell her mother in case her mother dabbed oil on her head as well.

"Elijah called by earlier this morning to see how you were." With that, Mrs. Miller left the room.

To whom had she been talking? *Was she talking to me or was she talking to Sarah?* Rebecca wondered. She also didn't want Elijah to see her like this. She imagined her nose was bright red and her eyes swollen from all the crying she had done the previous day. Sure, everyone always said it's what's outside that counts, but she still wanted to look good for Elijah.

Rebecca silently chastized herself once more. What was the point of looking good for Elijah? He was with Sarah now, not her. They might always stay friends, but it would not be the close friendship that the two of them had once enjoyed.

"I suppose Pirate is back at the Yoders' by now?" Esther asked Mrs. Miller when she brought in a tray laden under the weight of pot pie and set it between the girls.

"*Jah*, Mary and Elijah took Pirate home last night,

and then Elijah brought Mary back before he went on home. David was thrilled that Pirate's training had been sufficient for Pirate to find someone."

"He's a very clever dog," Sarah finally said.

Mary walked down the stairs, yawning and stretching. "Please forgive me, Mrs. Miller," she said. "I slept in. I'm sure it's the very first time in my life I've ever slept in."

Mrs. Miller waved her concerns away. "You had an eventful night," she said. "Of course it would have lasting effects. So, Mary, do you have a sore throat?"

"*Nee*," Mary said.

"What about a swollen throat? Or sinus trouble? Or a headache?" Mrs. Miller waved the bottle of peppermint oil at her.

Mary told Mrs. Miller she didn't have anything of the sort.

"Then sit with Rebecca and Sarah and I will fetch you some meadow tea with garlic. An ounce of prevention is worth a pound of cure." With that, Mrs. Miller walked out of the living room.

"What is the garlic all about?" Mary asked in a conspiratorial tone.

"I'm sure *Mamm* got the idea from Fannie Graber," Rebecca said, pulling a face. "Mrs. Graber always says said garlic's good for colds, so *Mamm's* put some in the meadow tea. It's a really horrible combination with peppermint."

"But it probably works for colds," Sarah said. "Didn't somebody say that medicine has to taste bad for it to work on you?"

Rebecca pulled a face. "Who said that?"

Sarah shrugged. "Someone. I'm sure I heard it somewhere."

Rebecca was awfully tired and her muscles ached, she presumed from being so cold and sitting in a cramped position against the fallen tree for so long. It was just a dull ache and not painful and she figured it would pass readily enough. Rebecca moved her chair closer to the fire.

"Are you cold?" Mary asked her.

Rebecca shook her head. "*Nee*, I just feel unsettled about getting lost last night."

"How *did* you get lost?" Mary said. "Surely you could find your way back?"

"*Nee*, it was quite scary, but at least I'm all right now."

There was a knock on the door and Mary had to hurry to answer it. She returned with Elijah. "Oh, you're both here," he said.

Rebecca could tell he looked disappointed. Maybe he thought only Sarah would be by the fire and perhaps he thought Rebecca would be asleep in her bedroom for the day after her ordeal. It was clear he wanted to speak with Sarah in private.

Rebecca stood up in a rather wobbly fashion. "I must see to something in the kitchen," she said walking away none too steadily.

"Allow me to help you," Elijah said.

"*Nee*, that's not necessary. You sit and chat with Sarah." Rebecca did not want to see Elijah's expression. She hurried in the direction of the kitchen, still clutching the blanket to her. When in the kitchen, she sat down at the old oak table and put her head in her hands. It was bad enough that Sarah and Elijah were now seeing each other, but to do it right under her nose? That certainly hurt.

Rebecca did her best to fight back the tears that were threatening to fall once more. *You must come to your senses*, she silently scolded herself. *Sarah lives here so you will see her with Elijah most of the time. You're going to have to get used to this and you're going to have to pretend you're happy for them.*

And Rebecca *was* happy for them, to a degree. But, her heart belonged to Elijah and she knew that would never change. Rebecca had a sudden good idea. She decided to go to Mary's community to live. With Sarah married Elijah, there would only be Rebecca and Mary left at the Millers' house. Mrs. Miller didn't need help anymore, so Rebecca could accompany Mary when she returned to her own community. Rebecca nodded slowly. Yes, that was a good idea, a good idea indeed. She would go to a new community and she would start all over again.

"It will be a fresh start," she said aloud.

Chapter Twenty-Six

Rebecca had spent a miserable week. In fact, it was the most miserable week of her life. Sarah was still acting strangely, presumably as she felt awkward about hiding her relationship with Elijah, and Rebecca was doing her best to be happy for the pair. After all, she blamed herself for not letting Elijah know how she felt about him. If she had done so years ago…yet Rebecca stopped herself right there. Like her *mudder* said, it was no use crying over spilled milk. What was done, was done. A dozen similar clichés ran through Rebecca's head, until she put an empty saucepan down rather too forcefully on the table. *Oh no, I'm turning into Mamm*, she thought.

Rebecca abandoned her work for the moment and walked to the door of the Miller *haus*. After *Grossmammi* Deborah's passing, Mrs. Flickinger had decided not to take in any new guests for the moment, and only had the one long-term guest, Benjamin Shetler. As a result, Rebecca had less work at the B&B.

The snow was falling again. Rebecca walked to the

edge of the porch and held out her hand, letting the snowflakes fall gently upon it. It looked like it would indeed be a harsh winter this year, with snow falling so early.

A buggy appeared through the snow, and pulled up outside the *haus*. Elijah climbed down, his handsome face illuminated by the threads of sunlight glistening through the snow.

Rebecca's heart stood still when she saw him. If only she hadn't been so silly; if only she had listened to the advice of the older women.

"Sarah isn't home," she pronounced, and then was surprised to see that her statement puzzled Elijah. He came to a stop and stood there, rubbing his chin, bewilderment in his eyes.

"I came to see you," he said, his voice faltering. "I wanted to speak to you about something."

A wave of misery washed over Rebecca. Clearly Elijah was going to break the news to her about him and Sarah. Well, she would do her very best to act pleased for them, never mind the fact that her heart was breaking. Rebecca realized that she hadn't responded. "*Jah*, sure," she said, with as much enthusiasm as she could muster.

"Would you come on a buggy ride with me?"

"What, now?" Not only was Elijah going to give her bad news, she was going to get frozen hearing it. "It's snowing."

"Only lightly. Why don't you get your coat and boots?"

Rebecca shrugged. "Okay, might as well get it over with."

Elijah scratched his head. "What did you say?" His handsome face was turned toward Rebecca, and she saw the worry there.

Rebecca clapped her hand over her mouth. She hadn't realized that she had spoken aloud. "Um, I'll go and tell *Mamm* where I'm going."

Rebecca returned to the buggy, silently lecturing herself to act pleased when Elijah told her he was dating Sarah. She couldn't let him see how she felt; that would be embarrassing. Besides, she wanted Elijah to be happy, although she would rather have him be happy with her than with Sarah.

The snow was falling gently as Rebecca took her seat next to Elijah. He reached over and wiped a snowflake from the tip of her nose.

I wish he wouldn't be so nice to me, Rebecca thought. *It just makes it harder.* Her heart beat rapidly at his touch. The thought that Elijah was going to marry another was too much. Rebecca feared she would break into sobs right then and there.

Elijah drove the buggy at a slow pace and turned into a little lane. The buggy wound its way down the lane, flanked by trees that looked as if they had been dipped in frosting. The snow was falling harder now, and Elijah placed another blanket over Rebecca's legs as he drove.

"I wanted to speak to you by the pond," he said, "but it's too cold out there now for us to get out of the buggy." He stopped the *familye* buggy and turned on the propane buggy heater that was mounted on the middle of the dash. The blue flame immediately sprang to light.

Elijah turned to Rebecca and twisted his hands nervously. "There's something I have to tell you."

Rebecca's heart went out to Elijah. As much as she was hurting for the news he was about to deliver, she couldn't bear him to be burdened by the weight of breaking the news to her that he was intending to marry Sarah. She sighed aloud. "Don't worry Elijah, it's all right, I know."

"You do?" Elijah's brows knit together in a frown. A snowflake drifted into his mouth and he sputtered.

Rebecca heard herself chuckle. It was as if she heard herself from far away. Her whole world was crashing down. She had known Elijah all her life; how would she ever manage without him?

Elijah was still speaking. "I don't think you do."

Rebecca simply nodded. He could no longer speak from sorrow.

"I've fallen deeply in love."

I know, Rebecca thought, wondering how long she could manage to keep her tears at bay.

Elijah frowned at her and chewed his lip. "I want to get married. How do you feel about that? I know we haven't actually discussed it. Oh dear, this is not the way I wanted to do it."

"Congratulations," Rebecca said, trying to look pleased for him.

Elijah rubbed his chin. "Rebecca, I'm serious. You don't seem to be taking this seriously."

To Rebecca's horror, and surprise, for she thought she had been controlling her emotions well, she burst into racking sobs. The next thing she knew was Elijah's arm around her. "Rebecca, whatever's wrong? You can say no. Please don't feel pressured."

"Of course I won't stop you and Sarah being married," Rebecca managed to get out through her sobs. "I'm happy for you both." She burst into a fresh bout of sobbing.

Elijah held her at arms' length. "Rebecca, look at me."

Rebecca took the tissue from her face and looked at Elijah.

"Whatever are you talking about?"

It was Rebecca's turn to be confused. "What do you mean?"

"I just asked you to marry me." His voice was soft and gentle.

Rebecca's world stood still. What had Elijah said? Were her ears deceiving her? "What, what about Sarah?" she stammered.

Elijah frowned and shrugged. "I don't know what you mean about Sarah. Why would I want to marry Sarah? I've always been in love with you."

Rebecca was trying hard to process the strange turn of events. The snow swirled more fiercely in harmony with her emotions. "But, the note you gave Sarah the other day, at the cemetery."

"The note? My *mudder* wanted someone else to sew for her at her quilt store. The note was from *Mamm* to Sarah to tell her she had the job. *Mamm* had a migraine the day of the funeral, if you remember."

"I remember, that's why she wasn't there," Rebecca heard her voice say. "But Nash Grayson told me that he saw you and Sarah kissing in the kitchen the day of the viewing, right after I left."

Elijah looked horrified. "I did no such thing! The nerve of Nash to say that. I knew he was up to something. Clearly he wants you for himself, so he was trying to drive a wedge between us."

Rebecca processed the information—yes, that did make sense.

Elijah took her hand. "Rebecca, my love, I've loved you all my life. Will you do me the honor of marrying me?"

Rebecca heard her voice again as if from far away, but this time, her voice was saying what she wanted it to say. "Yes, yes of course, Elijah. I've loved you all my life too."

"You have?" Elijah beamed. Rebecca's heart melted at the look of complete happiness on Elijah's face.

As the snowflakes swirled around them, Elijah's and Rebecca's lips met for the first time. She delighted in the softness of his lips and his gentle touch. Rebecca felt as if it were a dream, but it was a dream she never wanted to end.

* * * * *

SPECIAL EXCERPT FROM

When a television reporter must go into hiding, she finds a haven deep in Amish country. Could she fall in love with the simple life—and a certain Amish man?

Read on for a sneak preview of The Amish Newcomer *by Patrice Lewis.*

"Isaac, we have a visitor. This is Leah Porte. She's an *Englischer* friend of ours, staying with us a few months. Leah, this is Isaac Sommer."

For a moment Isaac was struck dumb by the newcomer. With her dark hair tamed back under a *kapp*, and her chocolate eyes, he barely noticed the ugly red scar bisecting her right cheek.

Leah stepped forward. "How do you do?"

"Fine, *danke*. Where do you come from?"

"California."

"Please, sit. Both of you." Edith Byler gestured toward the table.

Isaac found himself opposite Leah and gazed at her as the family gathered around the table. When all heads bowed in silence, he found himself praying he could get to know the visitor better.

At once, chatter broke out as the family reached for food.

"We hope you'll have a pleasant stay with us." Ivan Byler scooped corn onto his plate .

"I…I'm not familiar with your day-to-day life." The woman toyed with her fork. "I don't want to be seen as a freeloader."

"What is it you did before you came here?" Ivan asked.

"I was a television journalist," she replied. Isaac saw her touch her wounded cheek and glance toward him. "But after my…my car accident, I couldn't do my job anymore."

Journalist! What kind of God-sent coincidence was that? He smiled. "Maybe I should have you write some articles for my magazine."

"Magazine?"

Edith explained, "Isaac started a magazine for Plain people. He uses a computer to create it. The bishop gave him permission."

"An Amish man using a computer?"

"Many *Englischers* have misconceptions of how much technology the *Leit* allows," Ivan intervened. "You won't find computers in our homes, or cell phones. But while we try to live not *of* the world, we still live *in* the world, and sometimes technology is needed to keep our businesses running. So, some bishops have decided a little technology is allowed."

"What's the magazine about?" Leah asked.

"Whatever appeals to Plain people. Farming. Businesses. Land management."

"And you want *me* to write for it?" she asked. "I don't know anything about those topics."

"But that's what a journalist does, ain't so? Learn about new topics," Isaac replied. Her opposition made him more determined. "Besides, you're about to get a crash course while you stay here. Maybe you'll learn something."

"I already said I had no intention of being a freeloader."

He nodded. "*Gut.* Then prove it. You can write me an article about what you learn."

"Sure," she snapped. "How hard could it be?"

He grinned. "You'll find out soon enough."

Real estate developer Brittany Doyle is eager to bring the mountain town of Gallant Lake into the twenty-first century...by changing everything. Hardware store owner Nate Thomas hates change. These opposites refuse to compromise, except when it comes to falling in love.

Read on for a sneak peek at
Changing His Plans,
the next book in the Gallant Lake Stories miniseries by Jo McNally.

He stuck his head around the corner of the fasteners aisle just in time to see a tall brunette stagger into the revolving seed display. Some of the packets went flying, but she managed to steady the display before the whole thing toppled. He took in what probably had been a very nice silk blouse and tailored trouser suit before she was drenched in the storm raging outside. The heel on one of the ridiculously high heels she was wearing had snapped off, explaining why she was stumbling around.

"Having a bad morning?"

The woman looked up in annoyance, strands of dark, wet hair falling across her face.

"You could say that. I don't suppose you have a shoe repair place in this town?" She looked at the bright red heel in her hand.

HSEEXP0820

Nate shook his head as he approached her. "Nope. But hand it over. I'll see what I can do."

A perfectly shaped brow arched high. "Why? Are you going to cobble them back together with—" she gestured around widely "—maybe some staples or screws?"

"Technically, what you just described is the definition of cobbling, so yeah. I've got some glue that'll do the trick." He met her gaze calmly. "It'd be a lot easier to do if you'd take the shoe off. Unless you also think I'm a blacksmith?"

He was teasing her. Something about this soaking-wet woman still having so much…regal bearing…amused Nate. He wasn't usually a fan of the pearl-clutching country club set who strutted through Gallant Lake on the weekends and referred to his family's hardware store as "adorable." But he couldn't help admiring this woman's ability to hold on to her superiority while looking like she accidentally went to a water park instead of the business meeting she was dressed for. To be honest, he also admired the figure that expensive red suit was clinging to as it dripped water on his floor.

He held out his hand. "I'm Nate Thomas. This is my store."

She let out an irritated sigh. "Brittany Doyle." She slid her long, slender hand into his and gripped with surprising strength. He held it for just a half second longer than necessary before shaking off the odd current of interest she invoked in him.

HSEEXP0820